UNDER DURESS

David Brunelle Legal Thriller #18

STEPHEN PENNER

ISBN: 979-8-218-84917-7

Under Duress

Joy Lorton, Editor.
Cover design by Nathan Wampler Book Covers.

THE DAVID BRUNELLE LEGAL THRILLERS

UNDER DURESS

(1) In any prosecution for a crime, it is a defense that:

(a) The actor participated in the crime under compulsion by another who by threat or use of force created an apprehension in the mind of the actor that in case of refusal he or she or another would be liable to immediate death or immediate grievous bodily injury; and

(b) That such apprehension was reasonable upon the part of the actor; and

(c) That the actor would not have participated in the crime except for the duress involved.

(2) The defense of duress is not available if the crime charged is murder.

Revised Code of Washington 9A.16.060

CHAPTER 1

The blood was all wrong.

David Brunelle had been a prosecutor for more years than he cared to count and had worked homicides for too many of those. He knew how a murder scene was supposed to look. This wasn't it.

There was the standard pool of dark arterial blood, but it had been sliced and smeared like a dollop of red paint on a linoleum canvas. Crimson shoeprints and handprints littered the floor, overlapping with each other and with the crusted edges of the lake of drying blood, its width and breadth fully exposed to the central air of the medical building.

"The victim survived?"

Detective Larry Chen stepped over to Brunelle. "What was your first clue?"

Chen had been a detective longer than Brunelle had been a prosecutor, and he'd been working homicides a lot longer than Brunelle too. But enough of those homicides had been cases they had worked together that each knew they could rely on the other.

And how to rib each other too. "The fact that the body's gone?"

Brunelle grinned tightly. "Not that by itself. The medical examiner crew could have already collected the body. It took me longer to get here than it used to."

"That's what you get for moving to the 'burbs," Chen teased. "How's Casey doing, by the way? Bored with Bellevue P.D. yet?"

"She's good," Brunelle assured. "I think she likes the slower pace over there. But I'm still getting used to having to drive over the lake when I get that two a.m. murder scene call."

Chen checked his watch. "It was more like one a.m. You're getting old."

"Not as old as you," Brunelle returned. He pointed again at the bloody floor. "But the medical examiner folks would have been careful not to disturb the scene. By the time they're called, it's a murder investigation. But this scene is destroyed. The only excuse for trashing the scene this bad is if paramedics were trying to save the victim's life. Then you don't give a shit about the integrity of a crime scene. You're trying to save a life."

Chen nodded. "And the body's gone."

"And the body's gone," Brunelle finally agreed with a nod.

He took a step back from the thickening pool of blood and scanned his surroundings. They were in a small surgery theater, barely larger than a typical examining room. The operating table was actually a chair with multiple recline settings. Anatomical posters of various skin maladies adorned the walls. A tray of surgical implements had been tipped over, its contents scattered across the floor on the other side of the blood. Signs of a struggle, but not much of one. The single brass shell casing near the door suggested the struggle had been brief.

"If the victim is alive," Brunelle asked, "why did you call me? I don't remember the last case I handled with a live victim."

"He's alive," Chen confirmed, "but barely. I doubt he makes it through the night. It'll be a murder case soon enough."

"Planning ahead," Brunelle remarked with a pat on his friend's large shoulder. "I've always liked that about you."

Chen only replied with a grunt. Brunelle looked around the operating room again. "So, who's our victim? Some sort of doctor?"

Chen nodded. "Did you read the sign on the door when you walked in?"

"I did not," Brunelle admitted. "I was focused more on getting inside than the name of the business. The address you sent me led me to the parking lot. The crime scene tape led me the rest of the way."

"This is the office of Grunwald and Jacoby," Chen explained.

Brunelle just shrugged.

"The plastic surgeons?" Chen prompted. "They have ads everywhere. Billboards, the sides of buses, shopping carts. You haven't seen them?"

"I haven't noticed them," Brunelle answered. "I'm not looking to have any work done."

Chen grinned. "Give it a few more years. Casey's younger than you, right? You're going to want to keep up."

"She's not that much younger," Brunelle defended. "And she's not with me because of my looks."

"Lucky for you," Chen jabbed. Then he laughed and patted Brunelle back on the arm. "Sorry. I couldn't resist. Anyway, our victim is Harrison Jacoby. Shot and almost killed in his own business."

Brunelle frowned at the clock on the wall. "Well after midnight. What was he doing here? I doubt they were doing nose jobs at one a.m."

"Well, see, that's part of the mystery," Chen replied. "The other part is who called 9-1-1."

"Who?"

"His partner, William Grunwald," Chen answered.

"He found him?" Brunelle hazarded a guess.

"That's what he told the operator," Chen related. "Said there was a burglary in progress."

Brunelle glanced around the room again. "Who steals surgical equipment? I mean, maybe there's a secondary market for some of it. Sell it for drug money, I guess. Shoplifting a drill from Home Depot is probably a lot easier and worth just as much. Anything missing?"

"Yeah." Chen chuckled. "Any evidence of a burglary?"

Brunelle narrowed his eyes. "You think Grunwald did it?"

"We know he did," Chen answered.

"How?" Brunelle asked.

"Because he confessed when the patrol officers arrived," Chen explained. "He opened the door with the gun in his hand. He's lucky they didn't shoot him."

"Why didn't they?"

"He was holding it at his side, pointing down," Chen said. "They told him to drop it and he did. Then he said he'd killed his partner."

"Almost, anyway," Brunelle remarked. "Soon, I guess. So, it's not a who-dun-it. Should be easy enough for me to prove then."

Chen raised a cautious palm and unfurled a dark grin.

"Not so fast, Dave. You know it's never that easy. The case won't be about whether he did it. It'll be about why."

Brunelle frowned. He could feel the acid start spilling into his stomach. "Why?"

Chen waved his arm toward the hallway. "Why don't you ask him yourself? The boys have him detained in the conference room."

CHAPTER 2

The conference room for Grunwald and Jacoby, Plastic Surgeons, LLC, was designed for convincing aging professionals to spend their savings on time-delaying cosmetic procedures, not for interrogating would-be murderers. Rather than a spartan room with cinderblock walls, a squat metal table, no windows, and a two-way mirror for the prosecutor to watch the interrogation, the room boasted floor-to-ceiling windows with a view of Elliott Bay, steel and tempered glass furniture, and nowhere at all for the prosecutor to hide while the cops beat the confession out of Dr. William Grunwald.

But as it turned out, Grunwald was only too eager to confess, and without a beating. Almost without being Mirandized. Chen had to tell the good doctor to stop talking while he advised him of his constitutional rights. Brunelle took the opportunity to try to hide himself in the corner farthest from their suspect. He leaned back in his chair, crossed his legs, and placed a hand over the lower half of his face. He didn't need his mouth free. Chen would be asking the questions.

"And having been advised of your constitutional rights," Chen asked the final question before the real interrogation, "do you voluntarily choose to speak with me now?"

"I do," Grunwald replied enthusiastically, almost theatrically. "I absolutely do. I only hope you'll believe me."

Grunwald was the picture of a successful, middle-aged professional, fighting, rather well it had to be said, against the unstoppable onslaught of time. He had a thick head of black hair that probably would have been a receding hairline of gray without the hair plugs and hair dye. Taut skin was shiny on his cheekbones, obviously pulled back and stapled behind his ears. His teeth were unnaturally white, and his clean-shaven jaw was so square as to insist on its jaw point implants. Brunelle wondered if the cleft chin was a result of some Frankenstein-like procedure as well.

In truth, Brunelle had no idea whether Grunwald had had any of those procedures done. But he was a handsome man in his early fifties, and Brunelle allowed himself to feel a small solace at the idea that his comparative beauty might be store-bought.

"I hope I can believe you too," Chen replied. He was seated across the table from Grunwald, leaning forward enough to show engagement without betraying affirmation. "So, let's start at the beginning. You know the victim, Harrison Jacoby, is that correct?"

"Yes," Grunwald replied with a staccato of nods. "I killed him."

Chen sighed and leaned back. "That's not the beginning, Dr. Grunwald. That's the end."

A preview of the end, Brunelle thought. Jacoby was still alive.

"Don't you want to know why I killed him?" Grunwald

insisted, his voice cracking. "I had to do it."

Chen nodded. "That's what they all say, doctor."

Brunelle leaned forward and lowered his hand from his face. *A self-defense claim?* he wondered. There were really only two defenses to murder: I didn't do it, or I had to do it. The 'I didn't do it' went out the window when Grunwald opened the door to the cops with the murder weapon in his hand.

"But it's true," Grunwald almost wailed. "They were going to hurt my family if I didn't do what they said."

Brunelle flopped back in his chair. A third defense. Duress. "Shit," he hissed to himself under his breath.

Chen took a moment as well. He clearly wanted to go through the shooting, step by step, in chronological order. But he couldn't ignore Grunwald's efforts to control the conversation anymore. Not after that claim.

"Who was going to hurt your family?" he went ahead and asked.

Grunwald's mouth twisted into a crooked frown. "I don't know."

Chen raised an eyebrow at that assertion. "Someone coerced you into murdering your business partner, but you don't know who?"

"Yes." Grunwald nodded profusely. "That's it exactly."

"That's exactly not believable," Chen replied. "You might want to start over. Maybe try self-defense. A lot of people use that one. Of course, you shot him in the back of the head, so that might not be very believable either. Do you sleepwalk, doc? Maybe you could—"

"I'm not making up some excuse," Grunwald interrupted. "It's the truth. I don't know who they are, but they contacted me over the internet. They sent me pictures of my son at school. They said they knew his schedule, and they knew mine, and it would be easy to snatch him off the street when he was walking home from school."

Chen nodded. "Okay, okay. Let's go ahead and explore this. I have two questions right away. First, did you save any of these communications?"

Grunwald shook his head. "No. They told me to delete them immediately after I read them."

"Of course they did." Chen nodded again. "Okay, second question: do you have any idea why these people you don't know would want you to kill Dr. Jacoby?"

Another shake of Grunwald's head. "No. I tried to ask, but they told me they would be asking the questions. I was just supposed to do what I was told."

The perfect defense, Brunelle thought. *Completely unverifiable.*

"That's all very convenient," Chen responded. "The devil made me do it, but I don't know why, and I don't have any receipts. Sorry to have bothered you, Dr. Grunwald. Can I offer you a ride home? Maybe a letter of apology? How about a donation from the police union to your favorite charity?"

Grunwald's eyebrows knitted together, and he shifted in his seat. "I can't tell if you're joking."

"I am very much joking, doctor," Chen replied. "Let me tell you what I think really happened. I think you were stealing from the business and he caught you. Or *he* was stealing from the business and *you* caught *him*. Or one of you was screwing the other one's wife and got caught. I don't think there was some complicated and mysterious motive involving anonymous threats and deleted emails. I think this was just another attempted murder like every other case I've done for thirty years. Love and money are the biggest motives. I have no reason to believe this case is anything different."

Grunwald blinked at Chen for several seconds. Then, his chin quivering, he asked, "Did you say attempted murder? Harrison is alive?"

Brunelle frowned. He wasn't sure Chen should have given that information up just yet. He wasn't sure Chen meant to.

"He is," Chen confirmed. "He's in bad shape, thanks to you and that nine millimeter of yours, but when he wakes up, he's gonna tell us who was stealing from who, or who was fucking who. And then your dark-web blackmail story is going to fall apart like a Mexican butt lift."

Brunelle stifled a laugh. That didn't even make sense, but he liked the sound of it. Grunwald, less so, apparently.

"When Harrison wakes up," Grunwald responded, "he's going to tell you he has no idea why I would shoot him. Because I had no reason to. No one was stealing. No one was cheating."

Then Grunwald's eyes flew wide and he covered his suddenly gaping mouth with his hand. "Oh, my God. I failed. I didn't kill him. They're going to go after Kaeden." He tried to jump to his feet, but the heavy hand of the patrol officer behind him shoved him back into the chair. "You have to send someone to my house! You have to protect Kaeden!"

Brunelle raised his hand to his chin again. If Grunwald was lying, he was doing a hell of a job selling it. A jury would eat up that kind of performance.

Chen hesitated. Then he nodded to the patrol officer nearest the door. She nodded back and slipped out. It was subtle, but Grunwald noticed. "Thank you," he sighed and slumped into his chair.

"I still don't believe you." Chen jabbed a finger at his

subject. "I just want to see what your wife has to say about all this."

"Liz doesn't know." Grunwald sat up straight again. "She won't know what you're talking about."

"Of course not." Chen shook his head. "But maybe she also doesn't know how you suddenly could afford that vacation to Bali, or why you were working all those late nights when your partner was out of town, but his wife stayed home."

Grunwald hung his head and shook it. "I can't believe Harrison is alive."

Brunelle could hardly believe it himself. It had been a long time since he'd had a victim who could tell the jury what had happened to them. Speaking from the grave violated the evidence rules. He was looking forward to hearing what Harrison Jacoby had to say.

CHAPTER 3

Harrison Jacoby wouldn't be saying anything for some time.

"He's in a coma," the nurse informed Brunelle and Chen. "He may never come out of it."

Brunelle and Chen were at the ICU at Harborview Medical Center, the Level I trauma center for all of Washington State and four surrounding states as well. If Jacoby had been shot in the leg, he probably would have ended up at Swedish Hospital just up the street, like everyone else. With a gunshot to the head and a coma, he was at Harborview. At least it lived up to its name. It was perched on a hill overlooking Pioneer Square, Seattle's original downtown, and the southern end of the waterfront beyond. But the outlook for Jacoby was dim.

"Lost too much blood," Chen remarked. He had seen a lot in his career. He knew the causes of a coma, at least the ones that originated in violence.

Brunelle had seen a lot too. But not so much not to retain a whisper of hope. "Do the doctors think he'll pull through? I'd love to do an attempted murder case for a change."

"Why don't you ask me yourself?"

Brunelle turned to see a man he presumed to be Jacoby's attending physician, not least because of his comment.

"Dr. Kevin Martinson." The doctor extended his hand to both Brunelle and Chen. They each shook it as the nurse slipped out of the room and back to her rounds. "I hear you're from the police department?"

"He is," Brunelle jabbed a thumb at Chen. "I'm from the D.A.'s office. Dave Brunelle."

"And I'm Detective Larry Chen." A gesture toward Jacoby. "Is he going to make it?"

"Hm." Martinson grabbed his chin and stepped over to the hospital bed and its unconscious occupant. "An excellent question. I don't suppose you two gentlemen would be satisfied if I said that I hope so?"

"He might be," Brunelle answered. "His job is done. They caught the bad guy. Now it's my case."

"And is 'I hope so' good enough for you?" the doctor asked again.

Brunelle frowned. He considered the excuse Grunwald had given, the legal defense that excuse led to, and the limitations on that defense. "The shooter is claiming duress. It means he only did it because someone else forced him to, usually through a threat of violence against him or his family. But duress isn't available for murder. If Dr. Jacoby dies, it won't matter whether Grunwald was telling the truth when he spun that pretty unbelievable story he gave us."

Dr. Martinson frowned. "Does that mean you're hoping the patient dies?"

"No, duress isn't available for attempted murder either,"

Brunelle answered. "I mean, the statute only exempts murder, but the courts added attempted murder a long time ago. So, it doesn't matter if he lives or dies."

"It doesn't matter?" Martinson questioned.

Chen shook his head at Brunelle. "This is why everyone hates lawyers."

"Cops aren't exactly popular these days either," Brunelle returned. "What about you, doc? Do people still like doctors?"

Martinson shrugged. "I think it's case by case. They like us when we can give them good news."

"That sounds about right." Brunelle nodded. "We all work in a profession where we help other people with their problems."

"That sounds nice," Dr. Martinson remarked.

"It sounds stressful," Chen countered.

"It's probably both," Brunelle opined. "Anything worth doing is going to be stressful."

"I thought anything worth doing was worth doing well," Chen questioned.

"Doing it well is even more stressful," Brunelle replied with a grin.

He walked over to the bed and gazed down at the victim of his newest case. Jacoby had wires stuck to his head and chest, an I.V. in his arm, and a tube shoved down his throat. There were no perceptible signs of life. The only thing that insisted it wasn't a murder case—not yet anyway—was the notably slow beep of the heart monitor at the other end of one of those wires.

"So, tell us honestly, doc," Brunelle asked without looking up from the ashen face of Harrison Jacoby, "what are the odds he pulls through?"

"You mean to the point where he could sit and speak?"

Martinson clarified. "I assume that's what you're interested in. His ability to testify."

Brunelle shrugged. "Well, yes," he admitted.

"Don't worry. I understand," Martinson replied. "No judgment here. We all have a job to do. You can't do yours if our patient here can't tell the jury what happened to him."

"I can do my job without that," Brunelle assured. "In fact, that's sort of my area of expertise. But it will definitely be easier if I have a victim who can speak."

"Well, then," the doctor nodded, "I would say odds are probably about fifty-fifty."

"Not great odds," Chen observed.

Brunelle thought they could be worse. He had expected worse.

"Not even really odds," Martinson replied. "When I say fifty-fifty, I don't really mean there's some actual mathematical probability that in half of some possible scenarios, Dr. Jacoby wakes up and speaks again. What I really mean is that I don't know. I'm a doctor, not a mechanic, although there are certainly similarities to the jobs. But the human body is not a car. It has its own internal ebbs and flows that exist independent of what we can do. Everyone is different and everyone responds a little differently to different treatments. All I can do is give the patient the best chance to let their own body take over and heal itself. Will that happen in this case? I certainly hope so. But honestly, I don't know."

Brunelle was satisfied with that answer. He was also satisfied there weren't any more answers to be had that night. They would just have to wait and see whether Jacoby pulled through.

"Thank you for your time, doctor," Brunelle said. "Keep

us updated if anything changes."

Martinson agreed to do so, and Brunelle and Chen made their way to the lobby.

"I hate it when part of the case is uncertain," Chen said before they parted company. "I like to have it all locked down before I hand it off to you guys."

"I like that too," Brunelle nodded, "but it won't matter. Grunwald confessed and he doesn't get to claim duress either way. I mean," Brunelle appended, "unless the judge does something crazy."

"You lawyers and your exceptions to every rule." Chen shook his head. "I'd knock on wood, if I were you."

CHAPTER 4

"Did you knock on wood?" Brunelle's breakfast companion questioned a few hours later.

Casey Emory was a detective with the Bellevue Police Department, in Seattle's largest suburb. Bellevue was a tech hub with its own growing skyline of glass office towers and waterfront parks. There was less crime there, but it was only a matter of time before the growing community took on big city problems. Until then, Casey's caseload had a lot less murders than Chen's. That, along with the proximity of her house to the Bellevue Police Station and the fact that Brunelle had finally agreed to move into that house, meant she could occasionally enjoy breakfast with her prosecutor boyfriend.

"No," Brunelle admitted. "The entire office was glass and steel. I'm not sure there even was any wood to knock on."

"You're not sure because you didn't even try," Casey replied with a disapproving click of her tongue. "Cops can be superstitious, but we're not wrong."

Brunelle shrugged and bit off a piece of his toast. "If this were thirty years ago, I'd be worried. The duress statute only mentions murder as the crime it isn't available for, but the courts have expanded that to include attempted murder. It's settled law. Grunwald can't tell the jury he had to do it. I mean, he can, but they can't consider it. The truth is, he intentionally and premeditatively attempted to murder his business partner. It doesn't matter why."

Casey raised an eyebrow. "Motive doesn't matter?"

"Motive isn't an element," Brunelle replied. "The jury will want to know, but they can't acquit even if they agree with it. It's like that line from that comedy cop show. 'Cool motive, still murder.'"

"I dare you to say that in your closing argument," Casey laughed.

"I would," Brunelle returned, "but I don't think it's a very cool motive. Actually, I think it's complete bullshit. He didn't murder his partner because dark-web hackers threatened his family, and for no apparent reason, I might add."

"Why did he do it, then?" Casey questioned.

Brunelle grinned. "I don't know." He put the last of his toast in his mouth and washed it down with a swig of coffee.

"Aren't you curious?" Casey demanded.

"Oh, yeah, definitely," Brunelle confirmed after he finished swallowing. "Personally. It's always interesting why one person would kill another person. But I need to be careful professionally. I don't want to get into an argument about whether or not he acted under duress. Even if I win that argument, I could still lose the case. The jury won't be allowed to consider duress as a legal defense, but they're still human beings. If they think he's telling the truth, they won't want to convict him, and I can't appeal an acquittal."

He stood up to take his dishes to the sink. "The better play is to move to completely exclude any reference to the dark web story. Duress isn't a defense, so it's irrelevant. The jury may wonder what the motive was, but at least they won't be tainted by some sob story from a two-bit cybercrime novel."

Casey followed him into the kitchen.

"So, the jury will never know why this guy tried to kill his business partner?" Casey questioned. "Can you win a case like that?"

Brunelle frowned at her. "Don't you have faith in me?"

"I have faith enough in you," Casey answered. She set her plate on the counter. "I have a lot less faith in judges. Judges giveth and judges taketh away."

"Part of my job is to keep the judges in line," Brunelle responded, "and I'm very good at my job. I've got this."

Casey reached across the counter and grabbed a cutting board from its spot in the corner. She handed it to Brunelle. "Here."

Brunelle accepted it reluctantly. "Are we having something else? I kind of need to get on the road. I'm still getting used to the longer commute."

"It's wood," Casey explained. "You better knock on it."

CHAPTER 5

The judge's bench, as well as the counter below where the attorneys stood at the bar, were all made of wood. Brunelle hadn't really taken notice of that before. Not in the same way, anyway. He had declined to knock on Casey's cutting board—*their* joint cutting board, he had to remind himself—but he was beginning to wish he had as the hour for the arraignment approached. Bravado over breakfast was all fine and good, but winning an attempted murder trial against an intelligent and cold-blooded defendant was going to take every advantage he could muster.

Especially when that defendant had the resources to hire one of the best defense attorneys in Seattle.

Derek Milliken was the principal and sole owner of The Law Office of Derek Milliken, PLLC. He employed several associates, but they always introduced themselves on the record as, 'John Doe of the Law Office of Derek Milliken,' and 'Jane Roe of the Law Office of Derek Milliken.' They handled the lower-level cases that paid their salaries and covered the rent. Milliken himself rationed his court appearances for the biggest cases and richest defendants. Defendants like Dr. William Grunwald.

Milliken was in his early fifties, with thick black hair just beginning to gray at the temples. His strong chin was clean shaven, and he wore wire-rimmed glasses perched atop a slender nose. His suit was perfectly tailored, a dark gray with a subtle pattern, and his black leather shoes reflected the fluorescent lights above him. A crisp white shirt and silk burgundy tie completed the look of someone ready to release an attempted murderer back into the community.

Brunelle knew Milliken was there for the Grunwald case. There were no other cases scheduled on the docket that would have been worth his time. The judge wouldn't take the bench for a few more minutes, and the handful of other assembled attorneys were just making small talk Brunelle wasn't interested in anyway. He strode across the courtroom and extended his hand.

"Mr. Milliken? I'm David Brunelle, the prosecutor on the Grunwald case," he introduced himself. They had crossed paths, or at least brushed against each other's paths, over the years, but had never had a case against each other. He knew Milliken; he didn't assume Milliken knew him. "I assume that's the case you're here on?"

Milliken smiled broadly and shook Brunelle's hand vigorously. His grip was strong, but not overpowering. "Mr. Brunelle. A pleasure to see you again. Yes, Dr. Grunwald retained me to defend him in this matter. I look forward to providing a vigorous defense, and perhaps even convincing you to drop the charges altogether."

Brunelle smiled back, but not nearly as heartily. "That seems unlikely."

"Well, never say never, I always say." Milliken barked out

a laugh. "See what I did there? I do love an unexpected turn of phrase, don't you? Words are both toys and weapons."

Brunelle didn't have a response to Milliken's last statement, but then he didn't suppose it really called for one. Instead, he extracted copies of the charging paperwork and handed them to Milliken. "Here's the complaint. I'll go let the bailiff know we're ready to go first."

Milliken accepted the papers and agreed to Brunelle's suggestion. Brunelle crossed the courtroom and advised the bailiff that the big important case that had brought the cameras propped in the back of the courtroom was ready to go. Everyone would be happy to get the high-profile case handled so they could get back to the generally unobserved sausage making of the criminal justice system. There were two dozen other accused criminals waiting to be ground under the wheels of justice that afternoon.

The bailiff nodded at the information and checked off the case on his paper list of the afternoon cases, but declined to provide any audible response other than a low grunt that seemed directed more to himself than Brunelle. Milliken had already somehow managed to obtain one of the few seats at the side of the courtroom. Some young defense attorney probably recognized him and gave up his chair. Brunelle wasn't going to be receiving the same treatment, despite roughly the same number of years of experience. He stood against the opposite wall and awaited the judge's entrance.

"All rise!" the previously quiet bailiff called out. "The King County Superior Court is now in session, The Honorable Janice Atchison presiding."

Brunelle flinched at the name. The judges who handled the daily arraignment calendars were always rotating in and out.

None of them became judges to preside over preliminary hearings all day; they wanted to do trials. But the police still arrested people every night, so someone had to preside over the next day's arraignments. Brunelle just wished it weren't Atchison. Some judges hated prosecutors. Some judges hated defense attorneys. Some judges hated bailiffs, and court reporters, and jail guards. The Honorable Janice Atchison hated everyone.

"Be seated," she commanded. Her face held a perpetual sneer which matched her tone. She wore her black and gray-streaked hair in a tight bun and plastic-rimmed reading glasses hung on for dear life at the bulbous tip of her nose. Crow's feet bracketed squinty eyes. "What matters are ready?"

Brunelle pushed off the wall and stepped forward. "The matter of *The State of Washington versus William Grunwald* is ready, Your Honor. David Brunelle, on behalf of the State."

Milliken stood and approached the bar as well. "The defense is also ready on that matter, Your Honor."

He didn't introduce himself. He didn't need to.

"Mr. Milliken," Atchison greeted him with as much of a smile as she could muster. "Good to see you again."

Brunelle suppressed an eye roll. Being a financially successful attorney didn't just mean you had enough money for fancy suits and expensive shoes. It meant you had enough money to donate to judicial election campaigns. Atchison may have hated everyone, but she knew who to be nice to anyway.

"It's always a pleasure to appear before Your Honor," Milliken returned the saccharine.

The guard stationed inside the courtroom opened the metal security door to the holding cells with a loud clank and called for, "Grunwald!"

The good doctor might have been rich enough to hire Milliken, but he still had to spend the night in jail. At least until Atchison set his bail. Brunelle would try to get the number high enough to keep him in custody pending the trial, but he didn't find the exchange between Atchison and Milliken encouraging.

Grunwald entered the courtroom, dressed in red jail scrubs but otherwise looking well rested and in good spirits. Confident, even. He strode up to Milliken, shook his hand vigorously, and turned to face the judge.

"We are ready, Your Honor," Milliken announced.

Brunelle called the case for the record. "Good morning, Your Honor. We are on for arraignment in the matter of *The State of Washington versus William Grunwald*. The State is charging the defendant with one count of attempted murder in the first degree."

Brunelle handed the original of the criminal complaint to the bailiff, along with a summary of the alleged facts called the 'Declaration for Determination of Probable Cause.' Before a judge could impose bail on a defendant, they had to find that there was 'probable cause' for the crime charged—that is, assuming the truth of the State's evidence, ignoring any possible defenses, and drawing all reasonable inferences in favor of the State, could any jury possibly find the defendant guilty of the crime charged. It was a pretty low bar, and one easily met when the defendant confessed to the crime. Atchison would read it, find probable cause, and then they could argue about what the bail should be.

"The defense acknowledges receipt of the complaint," Milliken recited his lines, the verbal exchange every criminal attorney memorized after years and years of arraignments. "We waive a formal reading of the charges and ask the Court to enter a plea of not guilty."

"A plea of not guilty will be entered," Atchison completed the script, and the arraignment portion of the hearing was complete. Time for part two of two: the bail hearing. "I will hear from the parties regarding conditions of release. What is the State's recommendation, Mr. Brunelle?"

Typical bail on a completed first degree murder would be a million. Brunelle considered giving him a 25 percent discount for failing to finish the job, but that was due to incompetence, not mercy. "The State is asking the Court to set bail at one million dollars. I recognize this is not a murder case, but that's no thanks to the defendant. His intent was murder, and it is that intent which the Court should consider when weighing the factors for bail. By court rule, those factors are risk of flight and danger to others. Regarding the first factor, the defendant is a successful businessman who has the financial means—"

Brunelle threw a quick glance at the high-priced lawyer to his left.

"—to leave the country very quickly, a tempting course of action for someone with no criminal history who is now facing decades in prison. And especially after a taste of custody he experienced last night.

"As for danger to others," Brunelle continued, "it appears the defendant is a danger to anyone, even those closest to him. He attempted to kill a man who was his business partner for years and, until last night, apparently one of his closest friends. If he was able to put a gun to the head of Dr. Harrison Jacoby and pull the trigger, he is capable of doing that to anyone. Especially if it might aid in that flight I was just discussing."

Brunelle stole another glance at Milliken. He seemed entirely undisturbed. Almost amused.

"Therefore, Your Honor," Brunelle concluded, "for all of

those reasons, the State believes bail in the amount of one million dollars is appropriate and warranted. Thank you."

Atchison's standard scowl softened just enough to nod down in acknowledgment. "Thank you, Mr. Brunelle." She turned to his opponent. "I will hear now from the defense. Mr. Milliken?"

That bemused grin blossomed into a full, broad smile. "Thank you, Your Honor. I would like to begin by acknowledging Mr. Brunelle's passionate advocacy, and his accurate citation to the relevant authority, as delineated in the court rules. This Court must consider whether Dr. Grunwald is a risk to flee the jurisdiction and whether he is a threat to anyone should he be released. After that, however, I'm afraid Mr. Brunelle and I couldn't disagree more. Dr. Grunwald has hired me to fight the case, not flee from it. And he is no threat to anyone. Indeed, he was not truly a threat to his partner and friend, Dr. Jacoby."

That last line raised several eyebrows in the courtroom, not least of which were Judge Atchison's.

Milliken grinned again at the reactions he had elicited, then reached into his file and extracted several copies of a previously prepared document.

"I suppose now is as good a time as any to file this," he announced, and handed copies to Brunelle and the bailiff.

Brunelle read the caption. 'Notice of Affirmative Defense: Duress.'

"Duress?" he exclaimed, very much out of turn. "Duress isn't available for attempted murder."

"Yes, I hardly expected you to agree, Mr. Brunelle," Milliken responded, "but then again, I wasn't speaking to you. If I might continue, Your Honor?"

Atchison unfurled a disapproving glance at Brunelle, then looked back to the defense attorney. "Please do, Mr. Milliken."

What came out of Milliken's mouth next was a bit of a blur for Brunelle. He was far too focused on, and distracted by, the Notice of Duress paperwork to listen closely to whatever canned garbage Milliken tossed up on the bench.

"…no true intent to kill…"

Duress isn't available for attempted murder.

"…would never do anything like this willingly…"

Although the duress statute only excludes completed murder, not attempted murder.

"…immediately told the police what happened and why…"

The problem with case law changing the law is that judges can always change it back.

"…in fact, Mr. Brunelle himself was in the room when Dr. Grunwald explained how and why he acted under duress."

The sound of his name brought Brunelle back to the moment.

"Is that accurate, Mr. Brunelle?" Atchison questioned. "Were you aware the defendant claimed he was acting under duress from the very beginning of the investigation?"

The answer, of course, was yes. But Brunelle felt the fuller answer was that he might as well have been present when Grunwald asserted the defense of having eaten a peanut butter and jelly sandwich for lunch, or the sky is blue defense. According to the law as it stood in that moment, duress was no more a defense to attempted murder than Grunwlad's lunch or the color of the sky was. But Brunelle knew better than to say as much. Or at least, not in that manner.

"I have been aware of the defendant's claims since he

made them, Your Honor," he answered carefully. "I am also aware of the established case law that precludes duress from being a defense to the charge of attempted murder. I can assure you, my ethics would never allow me to charge a defendant with a crime I believe they are innocent of. And my ethics give me no regret for the decision to charge Mr. Grunwald with the crime he very much committed."

Judge Atchison's expression tightened. "I was not impugning your ethics, Mr. Brunelle. I was merely trying to ascertain whether you had at least some advance notice the defense might pursue this avenue."

Brunelle didn't entirely believe her, but he knew better than to pick a fight with a judge. She had climbed down a bit. He could do the same. "Of course, Your Honor. Yes, I am very aware the defendant wishes this defense were available to him."

Atchison accepted Brunelle's reply and turned back to Milliken. "Anything further on the issue of bail, Mr. Milliken?"

"Just that Dr. Grunwald looks forward to his day in court to prove his innocence under the law," Milliken responded. "I understand the Court is unlikely to release a defendant charged with attempted murder on his own personal recognizance, no matter how compelling the reasons to do so. While we would welcome such a decision from Your Honor, allow me to propose a bail amount of fifty thousand dollars. That is more than enough to impress upon Dr. Grunwald the importance of returning to court, but it is also an amount he can post so that he can be out of custody while we prepare his defense. Thank you."

Brunelle had to appreciate the advocacy. Milliken had thrown Atchison a bone. She could set bail but do so in such a nominal amount that it was functionally equivalent to a P.R. release. Judges loved a way out of the hard decisions.

And Judge Atchison adopted it wholesale.

"Bail will be set in the amount of fifty thousand dollars," she confirmed. "Further conditions of release shall be as follows. The defendant must appear for all future court dates. He must stay in contact with his attorney. He must have no violations of criminal law. And he shall have no contact with the alleged victim or the victim's family. Any questions?"

Brunelle had no questions. Not about the conditions of release anyway. He had significant questions about the notice of duress defense. But those were for a different hearing.

"No, Your Honor," Brunelle answered.

"None," Milliken concurred. "Thank you, Your Honor."

Brunelle didn't add his thanks to the judge, even as Grunwald showered them on Milliken. The guard was pulling him back toward the holding cells, but he'd be home in time for dinner. Brunelle had a feeling he'd be working through his own dinner that night. He should have knocked on wood.

CHAPTER 6

The only thing more troubling than trying to figure out why a smart and successful lawyer like Milliken thought he would be able to put forward a duress defense was trying to explain all of that to the victim's family. Which was exactly what Brunelle had to do immediately after the arraignment.

"Mr. Prosecutor! Excuse me, Mr. Prosecutor!"

Brunelle had reached the elevator bank but turned around to face whoever was calling after him. When he did so, he saw an absolute siren of a woman running toward him, arm raised, heels clacking, hair flowing. She wore a green bodycon dress, bunched up at a gold buckle on her left hip. Long platinum hair cascaded down her back, and gold chains adorned her wrists and throat. Her face was almost disturbingly perfect.

"Mr. Prosecutor, sir." She pulled up short when she reached him, out of breath from the effort. "I'm Veronica Jacoby. Harry's wife."

Brunelle knew he was a sucker for a beautiful woman. Luckily, this one had a husband. And he had a beautiful woman waiting for him at home anyway.

"David Brunelle." He extended a professional hand to shake. "Nice to meet you. I wish it were under better circumstances."

"Under different circumstances," Veronica responded as she shook Brunelle's hand awkwardly with only her fingers, "we wouldn't have met. Harry and I aren't really the types to hang out at dingy old courthouses."

Delightful, Brunelle thought. At least he was over being dazzled by the beautiful new woman.

"Can you explain what just happened?" Veronica asked. "And what's going to happen next?"

"Of course," Brunelle answered. He pressed the elevator call button. "Let's go to my office, and I can explain everything."

Veronica agreed and a few minutes later they were seated in Brunelle's dingy courthouse office. He sat behind the same government desk he'd sat behind for over a decade. Veronica sat across from him with implants far newer than that.

"So, that hearing we just conducted is called an arraignment." Brunelle leaned forward and clasped his hands on his desktop. "It's the first formal hearing in every criminal case, and its purpose is to inform the defendant of the charges against him. Now, you may have heard—"

"I don't really care about any of that." Veronica waved Brunelle's pedantry away. "What's going to happen to the business? Bill isn't going to get that is he? You can't inherit a business if you murder your partner, can you? I should inherit all of it, right?"

Brunelle leaned back in his chair again. That wasn't a line of questioning he had expected. Or was prepared to answer.

"Well, to begin with," he said, "your husband isn't dead,

so no one stands to inherit anything."

"He's not dead yet," Veronica responded. "But the doctors say it doesn't look good. Does it change things if he dies? Is that better?"

Brunelle considered Milliken's notice of duress defense, but decided not to tell the wife of the shooting victim that the legal case would be stronger if her husband died.

"It's never better if someone dies," he answered. "I'm sure we all want him to pull through and get back to his business and family as soon as possible."

Veronica didn't audibly agree. In fact, she frowned slightly.

"What exactly did the doctors say?" Brunelle asked. Whether it was 'better' or not, it would change things considerably if Jacoby died.

But Veronica just shrugged. "It was a lot of doctor talk, but it didn't sound like they thought his chances of a full recovery were very good. If he lives, he might just be a vegetable. Do people still say that?"

"I don't think so," Brunelle replied, "but I understand what you mean."

"How does that affect the business?" Veronica followed up rapidly. "I would have power of attorney or something, right?"

"So, here's the thing." Brunelle raised his palms to her. "I'm a prosecutor, not a business lawyer or an estate lawyer. I don't know how their business was set up and even if I did, I wouldn't know how that might be impacted by your husband's health condition. My expertise is criminal law. I know when someone commits a crime, and I know how to prove it beyond a reasonable doubt to a jury."

Veronica crossed her arms and frowned again. "Then I'm afraid you're not very helpful to me, Mr. Barnwell."

"Brunelle," he corrected, "and I'm sorry to hear you feel that way. You should probably consult a civil attorney. Someone with expertise in partnerships and long-term care planning."

"But if Harry dies," Veronica pressed, "Bill can't get the business then, right? You can't inherit a business or whatever if you murder the other person, right?"

Brunelle decided to venture an educated guess rather than plead ignorance again. He was ready to end the conversation, and he was confident enough in his answer to give her something to take with her when she left.

"That is correct. A murderer cannot inherit from his murder victim." Then, he felt compelled to add, "Let's just hope it doesn't come to that."

Veronica Jacoby did not look at all like she was hoping it wouldn't come to that. Brunelle considered Milliken's argument that the statutory text only excluded duress from completed murders and tried not to feel the same way.

CHAPTER 7

The next days saw Brunelle researching the duress issue. The next court date was the pretrial conference, exactly two weeks after the arraignment. It was when offers were made, counteroffers were proposed, and cases were settled. Some of them anyway. For the ones that didn't settle, the pretrial was when sabers were rattled, backs were raised, motions were filed, and trial dates scheduled. The Grunwald case was not going to settle. In large part because Brunelle wasn't going to offer anything. He attempted to murder someone. He could plead guilty to that or go to trial.

But setting for trial also meant setting a motion hearing to try to knock out that duress defense well before any jury could even smell it. The law seemed settled to Brunelle. But not to Milliken. That meant Brunelle needed to learn more about the law. Reading articles and studying cases. Legal research. He hated legal research. He much preferred the thrill of the courtroom over the monotony of a computer screen. But he didn't want to experience the wrong sort of thrill when his case collapsed at trial because he hadn't wanted to spend a few hours reading the legislative history of Revised Code of Washington 9A.16.060.

"Ugh." He put his head in his hands. "How am I supposed to argue against something that already isn't the law?"

A glance at the clock told him it had been nearly an hour since his last break, which had been a little less than hour after his previous break. Trial lawyers weren't good at sitting for long periods of time.

"Time for another coffee," he announced to no one but himself. He pushed himself out of his chair and gladly stretched his legs on his way to the elevators. There was a serviceable coffee shop on the first floor of the courthouse. It seemed to be on its third owner in as many years, but was hanging on. Brunelle would have thought there would have been a high need for caffeine in the courthouse, but then again, most of the lawyers, whether prosecutors or public defenders, were on government salaries.

"Tall Americano, please," Brunelle provided his order when he reached the front of the line.

"Room for cream?" the barista asked. She had blue hair and a nose ring, so he expected his coffee would be good.

"No, thanks," Brunelle replied, "but maybe throw in an ice cube or two to cool it down. I need to drink it as soon as possible."

"Weak," came a voice to his side, just out of view. He turned to see fellow prosecutor Gwen Carlisle shaking her head at him. "A real coffee drinker would just burn the roof of their mouth."

"That kind of coffee drinker only has scar tissue on the roof of their mouth," Brunelle returned. "I speak for a living. I can't risk my embouchure."

"Embouchure?" Carlisle laughed. "You're a prosecutor, not a clarinet player."

"Tall Americano." The barista announced Brunelle's drink before he could respond to Carlisle. "Kid's temperature."

Brunelle turned sharply to the barista, but she flashed a disarming smile and threw a wink at Carlisle. Brunelle decided not to be angry, but he didn't leave anything in the tip jar either.

"So, what are you working on that requires espresso in the afternoon?" Carlisle inquired as they both turned toward the elevators and their offices above.

She had been with the prosecutor's office long enough to have her own caseload of serious felonies, not least because of the experience she had gotten trying several murder cases with Brunelle. She was dressed for court, in a dark suit and silk blouse. She seemed to be letting her hair grow out a bit; the straight blonde strands brushed the top of her shoulders.

"New case," Brunelle answered as they both stepped toward the elevators. "Did you hear about that plastic surgeon who tried to kill his business partner?"

"Tried to?" Carlisle questioned. "He survived?"

"For now," Brunelle answered. "He's in a coma in ICU."

"So, you kinda hope he dies," Carlisle posited as she pressed the elevator button.

"Why does everyone think that?" Brunelle protested.

"Am I wrong?" Carlisle challenged.

Brunelle took a beat. "That's not really the point." He avoided the question. "The point is, the defendant told the cops he had to do it and then hired Derek Milliken, so now I've got a huge fight on my hands over whether duress is available for an attempted murder."

"It's not, right?" Carlisle ventured. The elevator arrived and they stepped inside. No one else joined them, so Brunelle felt comfortable continuing to discuss the case.

"Milliken is going to ask the Court to ignore the case law," Brunelle explained, "and go back to just the literal language of the statute."

Carlisle nodded approvingly. "Smart. Whenever the courts expand something it eventually retracts. Why not now and this case?"

"Whose side are you on?" Brunelle complained.

"Justice? I don't know. Something like that." Carlisle laughed.

The elevator doors opened and they stepped off into the hallway to the prosecutors' offices.

"What about you?" Brunelle changed the subject. "You look like you just came from court. Big case?"

"Meh," Carlisle answered. "Drive-by shooting, three co-defendants. No one died, but a few people got some extra holes in their bodies."

The receptionist buzzed open the secure door to the back offices, and they made their way toward Brunelle's office.

"Well, if you're not too busy, I may bounce this duress case off you after I do a bit more research," Brunelle said. "Milliken's good, and the judges like him. It might be a good case to have two prosecutors on. If you have the time?"

"I'll make the time for a murder case," Carlisle answered. "Oh wait. Your guy is still alive. Well, attempted murder is good too. And maybe we'll get lucky and our victim will die."

Brunelle was about to admonish Carlisle about bad karma, or at least tell her to knock on wood, when they turned the corner to see someone standing outside Brunelle's office. Not just any someone. Their boss, the elected county prosecutor, Matt Duncan.

"Uh-oh," Carlisle half-whispered and she pulled up short. "Looks like you're in trouble. I'm out. Good luck. But do bring me in on that case, if you don't get fired."

Carlisle retreated the way they'd come, and Brunelle was left to face their boss alone. But he wasn't worried about getting fired. He hadn't done anything worth termination—not recently anyway. He was just curious why his boss was darkening his doorway.

"Hey, Matt," Brunelle greeted him as he reached his office. Duncan was a little shorter than Brunelle, a little heavier, a little more worn down from years in the trial trenches followed by years dealing with politicians and the public. "To what do I owe the pleasure of your slightly intimidating presence?"

Duncan smiled, but weakly. "Don't worry, Dave. You're not in trouble. I need your help."

CHAPTER 8

Brunelle knew the answer to give. "Of course, boss. What do you need?"

"I need you to come with me," Duncan turned toward his office at the end of the hall. "Follow my lead and say as little as possible."

"I can definitely do the first two," Brunelle answered, falling into step behind Duncan. "No promises on the third one."

"I know," Duncan allowed. "But do your best. It could impact the job of everyone in this office."

Brunelle was taken aback by that comment. He was a cog in the machine, not the mechanic. He didn't want to be responsible for any cogs getting removed.

"What's going on?" he asked. They had almost reached Duncan's corner office, with its sweeping views of Elliott Bay and the Olympic Mountains.

"You'll see," Duncan whispered out of the corner of his mouth. "Now, smile, and pretend like a jury is watching."

The smile that popped onto Brunelle's face was genuine.

Duncan sure knew how to get a trial attorney to be on their best behavior.

Brunelle wasn't sure what he was expecting to find inside Duncan's office, but it wasn't the young woman standing at the window, her back to them as she took in the view. She had long shiny black hair, white pants that flared to cover most of the heels she was wearing, and a green sleeveless bouse that showed off tanned and toned arms. When she turned at their entrance, bright green eyes flashed out under dark eyebrows.

"Dave, this is Marietta Lang." Duncan commenced the introduction. "Ms. Lang, this is Dave Brunelle, one of our top homicide prosecutors. He's handling the case you asked about."

Brunelle took a step forward to shake Lang's hand, curious which case Duncan was talking about and why this woman he'd never met before would be asking about it, let alone why Duncan would respond to her inquiries by summoning him.

"Dave, Ms. Lang works for the State Auditor's Office," Duncan explained, obviously knowing Brunelle would be wondering exactly what he was wondering. "She's come to take a look at how we do things here."

Brunelle pulled his hand back from Lang and stifled a grimace. The last thing he wanted was for some state bean counter to come in and question how his office did things. No, actually the last thing he wanted was for some state bean counter to question how he personally did things.

"Pleasure to meet you, Ms. Lang," he knew to say.

"The pleasure is all mine, I think," Lang said with a barely concealed appraisal of Brunelle. "I like your suit."

"Uh, which case were you asking about?" Brunelle managed to ask.

"The William Grunwald case," Lang answered, her voice

deep and silky, like her hair. "It was all over the news this morning as I was driving up here from Olympia. I would love to get a chance to see how a high-profile case is handled from beginning to end. Especially if you're the prosecutor."

Brunelle wasn't sure what to say to that.

"That is," Lang added, "I think it will really give me some insight on how resources are used here."

Of course it was the Grunwald case. The one with the formidable opponent, the clever defendant, and the victim neither alive enough to testify nor dead enough to eliminate the threat of that duress defense.

"Wonderful." Lang's presence, mission, and affect had already made Brunelle forget Duncan's admonishment to say as little as possible. "I have to admit, though, I usually focus on justice, not costs."

A cool grin unfurled across Lang's thick lips. "You don't think the two can be related?"

"I don't think they should be," Brunelle answered.

"I think what Dave is trying to say," Duncan jumped in with a flash of a sideways glare at Brunelle, "is that we do our best to make sure people can't buy their way out of trouble. Take this Grunwald defendant for example. He's probably going to hire some expensive attorney to go up against our seasoned prosecutors."

"He already did," Brunelle informed them. "Derek Milliken."

Duncan's own polite smile slipped slightly. "Milliken? Oh."

"Yeah," Brunelle agreed.

Lang looked at the two men in turn. "Who is Derek Milliken?"

"Derek Milliken," Brunelle answered, "is one of the best, and most expensive, criminal defense attorneys in Seattle. Almost no one can afford him, but for those who can, he's the best lawyer money can buy."

"Does he get paid more than you?" Lang asked.

Brunelle couldn't stifle his laugh. "Oh yes. By a lot. I'm a government servant. He's a capitalist businessman."

"So, how do you beat someone like that?" Lang continued her inquiries. "Does getting paid better mean he's a better lawyer?"

"It doesn't mean that at all," Duncan answered. "Dave is a career prosecutor. He has dedicated his entire professional life to seeking justice for crime victims. You can't put a price on that."

Lang crossed her arms and smiled again. "I bet I can."

Brunelle knew she thought that was true.

"The other thing about our office," he said, "is that we're a team. We aren't just one lawyer, with only his name on the door, trying to make as much money as possible. Matt here is the boss, but it's not his name on the door. This is the King County Prosecutor's Office. Matt is the current leader, but he's a steward, not an owner. All of us are stewards. So, when a fancy lawyer like Derek Milliken walks into the courtroom, we can meet him with a team from our office."

"A team?" Lang asked. "You mean like more than one prosecutor? Do you do that?"

"All the—" Brunelle started to answer, but Duncan cut him off.

"Only when there are multiple attorneys on the other side," Duncan assured. "Usually. But even then, one of our experienced prosecutors is more than a match for an entire cabal of high-priced defense attorneys."

Brunelle liked Duncan's use of the word 'cabal,' but he wasn't a fan of the sentiment expressed with it. Especially when he had just recruited Carlisle to second-chair the Grunwald case with him.

"Okay, but the thing is—" Brunelle started to protest, but Duncan cut him off again.

"Why don't you take Ms. Lang back to your office and brief her on the case?" Duncan suggested.

Brunelle frowned at him, finally at a loss for words.

"Nothing privileged, of course." Duncan patted him on the shoulder. "Basic stuff. Summary of the facts. Expected defenses. Upcoming court dates. Things like that."

"I would love that," Lang remarked, "but how about just the upcoming court dates for now. I'm sure Mr. Brunelle has work to do. He is a dedicated public servant, after all. I can plan to come observe court." She smiled a bit too warmly at Brunelle, he thought. "I'd love to see you in action."

Brunelle found himself speechless for the second time. He regained his composure and managed to tell her the pretrial date. "I'm not sure there will be much to see. It's more of a conference between the attorneys than a hearing before a judge, but that's the next court date."

"I'm already looking forward to it," Lang answered. She turned back to Duncan. "Now, can we talk about payroll access? I'm going to need to compare service years with leave balances, and…"

Brunelle stopped listening and lingered only long enough to confirm with Duncan that he could leave. Duncan dismissed him with a thumbs-up and mouthed, 'Thanks.' Brunelle stepped into the hallway and felt like he could breathe again. He was proud of being a public servant, but he hated the administrative, even bureaucratic, side of government work. He just wanted to hold the bad guys responsible. Especially privileged bad guys like William Grunwald.

Too bad Carlisle couldn't help him do it after all.

CHAPTER 9

"That's bullshit." Carlisle slammed a fist down on her desk at the news.

Brunelle could hardly disagree. But he could try to explain. "I think Matt was just nervous about looking wasteful."

"Why didn't you say something?" Carlisle demanded. "Stick up for me? For justice, or whatever."

"I don't know." Brunelle shrugged. "I guess I was distracted by everything."

Carlisle took a moment, her eyebrows converging. "Oh, no. She's hot, isn't she?"

"Uh," Brunelle hesitated. "No?"

"Damn it." Carlisle shook her head. "You're too old for that shit, Dave."

"Look, I'll get you on the case," Brunelle promised. "Just let me do the pretrial by myself, and I'll explain to her the advantages of having two prosecutors on an important and complicated case. I didn't really get a chance to do that yet."

"Because you were staring into her baby blue eyes?"

Carlisle alleged.

"No." Brunelle crossed his arms. "And they're green, not blue."

Carlisle laughed. "Tell her you need a woman on the team to distract all the men on the other side. She'll understand that."

Brunelle cocked his head at her. "You're gay."

Carlisle laughed. "So what? Milliken isn't."

Brunelle supposed she had a point. But Duncan had made a point too.

"I'll make it happen," he told her. "By the time I'm done dazzling Marietta Lang at the pretrial, she'll be asking me how we can possibly afford not to put you on the case."

"Because I'm awesome?" Carlisle prompted with a smile.

"Sure," Brunelle allowed.

"And I'm the one who said you need to figure out why Grunwald really shot his business partner in the head?"

"Uh, yeah," Brunelle agreed.

"And have you figured out how you're going to explain to your cop girlfriend why you listened to me but not her?"

Brunelle sighed. "Well, no, actually," he admitted.

Carlisle nodded. "Dazzle Casey first, Romeo. I can wait."

* * *

"Hi, honey. I'm home!" Brunelle called out as he stepped into what recently became his shared home with Casey. He still wasn't used to driving to the suburbs and walking in the front door of a stand-alone house. He wasn't sure he was happy about it either.

"In the kitchen!" Casey called back to him.

Brunelle dropped his briefcase on the shoe bench and hung his jacket on one of the hooks by the door. He made his way through the living room to the kitchen. "Cooking already?"

"Nope," Casey answered. "Making a drink. Want one? I can whip you up a Manhattan before we order takeout."

"Takeout sounds good," Brunelle answered. He didn't need to confirm the drink; Casey had already pulled a second glass out of the cupboard.

"Long day?" Casey asked as she poured the bourbon.

Brunelle shrugged. "Complicated."

"Did you recruit Gwen onto your new case?"

"That's one of the complications," Brunelle answered. "Not yet, but I'm working on it."

"Mm-hmm." Casey handed him his drink. "But you did run the case past her, right?"

"Right," Brunelle confirmed.

"And she told you I was right, didn't she?" Casey grinned over her glass. "About needing to prove the real motive."

Brunelle took a sip then nodded. "Yes," he admitted.

"And," Casey tipped her glass toward him, "you listened to her even though you didn't listen to me. Isn't that also true, Mr. Brunelle?"

Brunelle took another drink, then lowered his glass. "You'd make a good lawyer, Detective Emory. That's excellent cross-examination form."

"So, that's a yes?" She didn't let go.

"That's a yes," Brunelle admitted with a sigh. "Are you upset?"

"I'm used to it," Casey avoided answering directly. Brunelle could tell she seemed hurt at least. "But that means I can anticipate it too."

She gestured toward the living room. "I made a list of ten possible motives. It's on the coffee table. Take a look while I put in the food order. I hope you want Thai food because that's what we're having."

"Thai is great," Brunelle knew to answer. He crossed back into the living room where he sat down on the couch and picked up Casey's list of possible motives Dr. William Grunwald might have had for trying to murder Dr. Harrison Jacoby.

"Let me know which motive you like best," Casey called out from the kitchen. "Or we could get Gwen on the line and she could pick one. I hear she's usually right about this sort of thing."

Definitely upset, Brunelle thought to himself.

He began reading the list while he waited for Casey to join him. A few minutes later, the food was ordered and Brunelle had run through all of Casey's theorized motives.

"So, which one do you like the most?" Casey asked as she dropped down on the couch next to him. "I'm partial to number three."

Brunelle read it aloud. "'Three: Grunwald having affair with Jacoby's wife.'"

"What do you think?" she asked.

"I don't know," Brunelle answered. "I met her. I didn't like her, but she didn't seem like she cared about Grunwald. She was only interested in which way the money was going to flow."

"What about number four?" Casey asked. "Too obvious?"

"Four: Jacoby having affair with Grunwald's wife," Brunelle recited it. "I like that one better. Simple revenge. But I didn't get that vibe from him either."

"Of course not. He was lying to you," Casey pointed out.

"Fair point," Brunelle conceded. Then he decided to address the upset elephant in the room. "I'm sorry I listened to Carlisle and not you. I mean, it was really that she confirmed what you said, so it's like I did listen to you too, I just needed multiple people to say—"

"Stop apologizing, Dave," Casey interrupted him. "I know who you are. It's just the cost of doing business."

Brunelle frowned at her. "What does that mean?"

"It means if you like someone enough to spend most of your time with them," Casey explained, "there are going to be things you maybe don't like so much. But you can't expect the person to stop doing those things because they're part of who they are and you like who they are, for the most part. So, things like leaving wet towels on the floor or not replacing the toilet paper roll, those are annoying, but if everything else is good, then those annoyances are just the cost of doing business."

Brunelle thought for a moment. "Do I leave wet towels on the floor?"

Casey laughed. "No! What you do is discount what non-lawyers say because they aren't lawyers. It's annoying, but it's predictable, and I knew that before we moved in together. Sometimes I wish it were just wet towels on the floor. Although not replacing the toilet paper might be a deal-breaker."

Brunelle nodded. "Agreed."

"I knew I was right, even if you didn't yet," Casey continued. "So, I let you go off to Lawyerland and talk with your lawyer pals. In the meantime, I did my detective thing and made a list of possible motives that I knew you'd be ready for eventually."

Brunelle looked at the list again. It was a good list. But he didn't think any of the motives on it were quite right.

"I bet it was number three," Casey said.

"Yeah, maybe," Brunelle hedged.

"No, I mean, seriously, I'll bet you." Casey stuck out her hand to shake. "I bet you it was number three. Grunwald was having an affair with Jacoby's wife, and they planned the murder.

Then he would get the entire business, and they could run off together."

"What do you get if you win the bet?"

Casey pointed at him. "You agree we move this relationship to the next step. It took forever to get you to move in with me. We're both in our forties, so kids? Probably not. But dying alone? Definitely possible. I'd like to avoid that, and I'd like to avoid that with you."

Brunelle took a moment to make sure he understood what she was saying. "You want to get engaged on a bet?"

Casey smiled. "You're already married to your job, Dave, so I know the only way to get you to marry me is to link that decision to your work."

Brunelle looked down at Casey's hand, a hundred thoughts flying through his head and enough wisdom to know not to voice any of them in that moment. "I don't know what to say."

"Say it's a bet," Casey answered. "I may be crazy, but that's the cost of doing business with me."

Brunelle smiled. "I do like doing business with you." Then he shook her hand. "It's a bet."

CHAPTER 10

The challenge wasn't going to be coming up with a plausible motive. The challenge was going to be uncovering the actual motive. Whether or not it was what Casey had wagered the future of their relationship on. Brunelle was willing to leave that to fate. But if he was going to give the jury a counter-narrative as to what Grunwald's true intentions were, it had to be iron clad. If Milliken poked even one hole in it during the trial, the jury would fall back on Grunwald's bullshit duress claim and acquit the bastard.

The problem lay in the fact that only one person knew the truth: Grunwald himself. The hope lay in the fact that Grunwald almost certainly told his lawyer. Which meant, when the pretrial came around two weeks later, Milliken had the truth inside his head and would be trying to keep it hidden. Brunelle just needed to speak carefully to listen closely.

A goal complicated by the presence of a non-lawyer, Marietta Lang. At best, her interests that morning were different from Brunelle's. At worst, they were antagonistic to his. Brunelle had done his job long enough to know to always expect the worst. But he also knew how to turn a difficulty into an advantage.

"Explain to me again what this court hearing is," Lang requested as they made their way from Brunelle's office to the room all the lawyers called 'The Pit.' It was a large conference room filled with too many lawyers and not enough chairs. There was a courtroom connected at the far end, in case a judge was needed to sign off on a scheduling order or something equally uninteresting, but the real action was in The Pit.

"It's probably easier just to show you," Brunelle answered. He opened the door to The Pit with his security badge and held it for Lang to walk in first.

Inside was a cacophony of frenetic energy. Dozens of prosecutors and defense attorneys connected and separated again to negotiate their cases. One defense attorney might have ten cases with seven different prosecutors. One prosecutor might have three cases with three different defense attorneys. It was like a bar full of speed-daters in suits and carrying armfuls of files. In between the negotiations were stories about weekend adventures and pictures of kids growing up way too fast. A lot of them went to law school together; some of them had known each other for decades. Professional adversaries with personal friendships. Enough so, that they would routinely shout out their own opinions about negotiations not their own, but close enough to overhear.

"That's a terrible offer!"
"You better take that offer."
"What about two for one?"
"Can you knock off another year?"
"You should just take your chances with a jury."
"You can get better than that at trial."

"The jury is gonna hate your client."

"The jury is gonna hate your victim."

Lang appeared duly impressed. Or shocked, maybe.

"Is it always so…" she searched for the word, "chaotic?"

Brunelle shrugged. "It's organized chaos."

Lang gestured at the activity. "It reminds me of those videos of the trading floor at the New York Stock Exchange."

Brunelle stuck out his lip and nodded. "I suppose so. It's the same thing, basically. Wheeling and dealing. Only instead of dollars, we deal with years in prison."

"Wow." For a moment Brunelle thought Lang had finally realized how significant their work was. How far beyond simple numbers. "Is it effective?"

"Oh yes," Brunelle assured her. "We can get more done in a couple of hours here than we could in a week of emails."

"Still," she raised a hand to her chin, "I bet there are ways to increase efficiencies."

Brunelle sighed to himself. "Come on," he suggested. "Let's find Milliken."

Lang had worn a navy suit that day, presumably to blend in with the attorneys. Brunelle suspected her happy disposition would give her away.

"Who's the new gal?" asked one of the very first attorneys they passed. He stuck out his hand. "Nick Lannigan, defense attorney. Don't believe anything Dave told you about me."

"I promise I didn't even think to mention you to her," Brunelle replied. "This is Marietta Lang. She's with the State Auditor's Office."

"Oh!" Lannigan pulled his hand back with faux concern. "Budget cuts, huh? Well, no worries. I'm private. If there are less public defenders, that just helps me."

"Less prosecutors means less cases filed," Brunelle returned. "Less cases means less work."

Lannigan pointed a finger-gun at Brunelle. "Good point." Then to Lang, "Only cut public defender jobs, please."

"I'm not here to cut any jobs," Lang insisted. "I'm just here to evaluate processes. Criminal justice is no different from any other government service."

Brunelle thought it was very different from any other government service, but he kept his opinion to himself, for the time being anyway. He extracted them from the conversation. "Nice to see you, Nick."

"He was friendly," Lang commented as they pushed deeper into the crowd.

"A lot of private defense attorneys are," Brunelle replied. "It's how they try to get deals."

"Does it work?" Lang asked.

"Not on me," Brunelle answered. He pushed away thoughts of past friends and lovers from the defense bar. Until he ran into one of those friends standing in their way, and a good enough friend he couldn't not say hello.

"Jess," he drew the woman's attention away from the prosecutor she was browbeating. "I'd like to introduce you to Marietta Lang. Marietta, this is Jessica Edwards, one of the best of those public defenders Mr. Lannigan suggested you fire."

"Nick wants public defenders fired?" Edwards shoved her hands on her hips, her blond hair swinging over her back again. She was wearing a suit similar to Lang's, but any sunny expression had been lost to years of defending the worst people against the most serious charges. Even when she smiled, like then, it was usually sardonic.

"He wants more business," Brunelle explained.

"Of course he does," Edwards replied. "Some of us are in it for more than money."

Edwards was what the prosecutors pejoratively called a 'true believer.' Brunelle liked her anyway.

"Nice to meet you, Ms. Edwards," Lang finally got a word in. "I'm sure someone from my office will be contacting yours soon, if they haven't already."

"And I'm sure my boss will tell them to fuck off," Edwards replied with another of those sardonic grins. "We always have to make do with less than we need. Part of the job when the public thinks you're the bad guy."

Lang didn't seem to know what to say to that. Brunelle did.

"See you later, Jess. It's been too long since we had a case against each other."

"I'm sure that'll change soon," Edwards replied. "Nice to meet you, Marietta."

They pushed on past Edwards and finally spied Milliken. He was sitting in the corner, at one of the few tables provided. He was the sort of lawyer who showed up early. Brunelle was more of a 'just in time' sort of lawyer.

"Mr. Brunelle." Milliken stood to greet them. "It appears you have co-counsel. Worried you can't beat me alone?"

"Not in the least," Brunelle returned. "And certainly not on this case."

Lang leaned in to offer her hand and introduce herself. "Marietta Lang. State Auditor's Office."

"Oh." Milliken's eyebrows shot up. "Well, I can assure you, Ms. Lang, this case is an absolute waste of taxpayer resources. My client is innocent and has an ironclad defense."

Brunelle looked to Lang. "His client shot a man in the

head, and his defense doesn't apply to the charge." He turned back to Milliken. "She's not here to manage my case, Milliken. She's just observing."

"So, please," Lang spread her hands out and took a step back, "do your jobs, and I will observe."

Easier said than done, Brunelle thought. Having an observer—a witness—couldn't help but impact how anyone did anything. Brunelle negotiating a case was no different. At a minimum, he would probably swear less.

As for Milliken, there were two general possibilities. One, he would freeze up and say less than Brunelle needed him to. The other, and far more likely, option was that Milliken would feel the warmth of an audience and not be able to help himself from performing, which would include an increased level of loquaciousness. At least, that's what Brunelle was hoping for. It was why he'd agreed to bring Lang along.

He just needed Milliken to let one thing slip. Anything. Then Brunelle would know which of Casey's ten possible motives was the real one. He didn't let himself dwell on which one he hoped it was—or wasn't.

"Okay, Derek." Brunelle crossed his arms. "I'll give you a chance to convince me. Even if it's legally a defense against attempted murder—and it's not—I do care if your guy acted under duress. Who was threatening his family, and why?"

Milliken sat down again, slowly, and looked up at Brunelle with a grin. "Well, that's just it, Mr. Brunelle. Dr. Grunwald has no idea why someone wanted Dr. Jacoby dead. I imagine Dr. Jacoby would know best."

"Your client put Jacoby in a coma," Brunelle pointed out.

"So it would seem," Milliken agreed. "Then perhaps ask Mrs. Jacoby. That is, if she is actually aware of all of her husband's dealings."

Brunelle nodded several times as he considered Milliken's opening gambit. He was going to turn the tables and accuse Jacoby of some uncertain malfeasance. Jacoby was in no condition to defend himself, and the fact that his wife didn't know about it was just evidence of how bad it all was.

"Your client's computer," Brunelle prompted with a new subject.

Milliken smiled broadly and looked up at Lang. "This is why they gave the case to Mr. Brunelle. He's one of their best. I'm sure he already knows that Dr. Grunwald's laptop has no evidence on it. Dr. Grunwald was instructed to delete all communications from the blackmailers or risk the safety, nay, the very lives of his family. He did as instructed, as any loving husband and father would. And that's why the police found nothing of value when they searched it." He looked back to Brunelle. "Isn't that right?"

Brunelle hadn't received the computer forensics report yet. But he was comfortable that Milliken knew the truth. "Right," he agreed.

"Shall I pitch our duress defense to you again," Milliken took on a weary affect, "or shall we just go ahead and set the case for trial? We can schedule a motion hearing to determine in advance whether I will be allowed to present a duress defense to the jury. I'm confident in the result, but it's always nice to have those sorts of things squared away before opening statement. I doubt you'll be willing to dismiss the case today based just on my word," he threw another grin toward Lang, "although that would save the taxpayers a lot of money."

"I'm salaried," Brunelle shot back. "I don't get paid by the hour like you. I might as well try your case as any other."

"I guessed you'd say something to that effect." Milliken frowned. "For you, it's just a job. For Dr. Grunwald, it's his entire life."

"It's Dr. Jacoby's life, too," Brunelle returned. "Which is hanging by a thread thanks to your client. You can save me the sob story. The only one getting rich off of this tragedy is you."

"Don't forget Mrs. Jacoby." Milliken's grin returned. "She stands to gain the most if her husband dies and my client goes to prison. I bet she knows more about this whole sordid affair than she's letting on. In fact, maybe she's the one who was sending the emails to Dr. Grunwald. Wouldn't that be a twist?"

Brunelle didn't respond. He'd gotten what he came for. It was time to end the interaction. "Let's set it for motions in a month and trial a month after that. The sooner the better." He threw his own glance at Lang, to use her to defuse the directness of his proposal. "Before my funding gets cut."

Milliken laughed a bit too hard at the joke. "Excellent." He extracted a paper from his briefcase. "While I was waiting for you, I took the liberty of filling out the scheduling order. We can just add those dates and have the judge sign off on it."

Brunelle took the order from Milliken and added the dates for the motion hearing and the start of trial. They wouldn't know which of King County Superior Court's fifty-two judges they would be in front of until just before the hearing. It would depend on what else was going on in the courthouse and who might be available. Such was the lot of practicing in the largest court in the state.

They dropped the paperwork in the basket for agreed scheduling orders. The judge would sign it and all the other orders at the end of the morning once the basket was full. That concluded the pretrial. Milliken packed up his briefcase. Brunelle led Lang through the still crowded room and into the hallway.

"That didn't seem to go well for you at all," she remarked once they were outside The Pit.

"That's because you're not a lawyer," Brunelle answered. "In my opinion, it couldn't have gone better."

CHAPTER 11

"Who did the forensic analysis of the computer?" Brunelle demanded. "What did they find? What didn't they find? Why and why not?"

Chen raised his palms at his unexpected visitor. He was seated in his office chair. Brunelle was leaned halfway over his desk. "Whoa. Calm down, Dave. One question at a time. First of all, I assume you're asking about the Grunwald case?"

"Of course." Brunelle stood upright again. "What else would I be here about?"

"We both have more than one case, Dave," Chen answered. "You want me to run a statistical analysis to see how many you and I have in common? I bet it's more than one."

"Only one involves a laptop that supposedly sent the shooter secret threats to make him commit the crime," Brunelle responded. "I don't give a shit about anybody's laptop if it's a drug deal gone wrong or two twenty-something duds at a bar with too much beer in their guts and too many guns in their waistbands. Yes, the Grunwald case."

Chen lowered his hands again and nodded. "Okay. Good. Just let me pull up the case file and I'll see who did the computer analysis." He turned to his computer monitor and clicked his mouse several times. After a few moments, he chuckled. "It was Houser."

"Why are you laughing?" Brunelle frowned.

But Chen grinned. "Because Houser is our best. Juries love him. But I don't know why he's still a cop."

Brunelle wondered what that all meant, but he supposed he'd find out soon enough.

"Come on." Chen stood from his chair. "He should be down in the forensics lab."

* * *

The computer forensics lab for the Seattle Police Department was located in the basement of the downtown precinct, the same building that hosted the major crimes unit and Chen's office. It was a short elevator ride and Brunelle was standing face-to-face with Jack Houser, Seattle PD's preeminent expert on electronic data storage and recovery.

Brunelle had expected a scrawny nerd. Houser was anything but. He was on the shorter side, but with an athletic build and large biceps. Tanned skin, white teeth, and long sandy blond hair gave the impression of a surfer, not a tech wizard. But when he started talking about his work, the nerd came out.

"The Grunwald case?" he practically sang. "Oh, this is a great one. Singular. Unique. I am absolutely loving what I'm finding."

Brunelle liked the sound of that until Houser added, "I mean, you're going to hate it. But I love it."

"What's so great about the case?" Chen asked for Brunelle. "I mean, for you?"

Houser smiled and nodded. "Come here. I'll show you."

He led them to a workstation on the far side of the lab. It would have been a cubicle but there weren't even the temporary half-walls that cubicles usually had. It was just a stool and a table, with a closed computer laptop on it.

"Is that Grunwald's computer?" Brunelle asked, pointing at the laptop.

"It sure is," Houser seemed happy to say. "I've been doing some extra tests on it before I finish with it."

That explained why Brunelle didn't have a report back yet. And confirmed Milliken's assertions about what they would find on the computer came from what Grunwald told him, not what Houser figured out.

"So, what's the headline?" Brunelle asked. "Not to cut the presentation short, but I'm a lawyer, not a tech guy. What's so interesting about the computer?"

Brunelle had worried Houser might be a bit put off by Brunelle's attempt to short circuit his presentation, but Houser just grinned wider and pointed two index fingers at Brunelle. "Let me ask you a question, Mr. Prosecutor. What are you hoping to find on this device?"

Brunelle thought for a moment. "Me? Nothing. Nothing special anyway. It's the defense who claims the shooter received a bunch of threatening emails that pushed him into trying to kill his business partner. But they were quick to claim that he deleted all of the emails. So, I don't know what I'm hoping to find, but I'm expecting to find nothing. The defense attorney says there's nothing because his client deleted it. I think there's nothing because they're making it all up in the first place. So, which is it? Can you even tell?"

"Oh, I can tell," Houser answered, shifting his weight

excitedly. "And it's neither of those things. Well, not exactly. It's not what you think, and it's not what they claim."

That sounded about par for the course, in Brunelle's experience.

"Cut the riddles, Jack," Chen interjected. "Just tell us what you found."

"Nothing," Houser answered. "I found nothing. And I should have found something."

Brunelle pinched the bridge of his nose. "Can you explain it to me like I'm not a computer forensics expert? Like I'm a regular person. Like I'm a juror. Because that's what I'm going to need to do."

Houser nodded several times, mostly to himself. Then he grabbed the trash can off the floor and slammed it on top of his workstation. "Okay, see this garbage can?"

"I can hardly not," Brunelle replied after the dramatic maneuver.

"Right," Houser acknowledged. "Imagine this is the trash can icon on your desktop."

"Okay." Brunelle nodded. It was precisely that: a trash can on a desktop.

"Now, imagine I have some file," Houser said. He scanned the top of his desk, then the next one over and found what he was looking for. He grabbed a blank piece of paper. He shoved it toward Brunelle. "Here. Take this and write something on it. Email, complaint, letter to grandma. Doesn't matter."

"How about an email with the criminal complaint against grandma attached?" Chen suggested, unhelpfully.

"Fine," Houser agreed quickly.

"I'll write email," Brunelle said with a sideways glance at Chen. He pulled a pen from his jacket pocket and scrawled the word across the page. "That's what I'm focused on in this case."

"Perfect." Houser pointed at the garbage can. "Now put it in the trash."

"Delete it?" Brunelle suggested, raising the paper toward the top of the trash can.

"Exactly," Houser nodded. "Put it in the trash can."

So, Brunelle let go of the piece of paper and it fluttered to the bottom of the receptacle.

"Fantastic!" Houser exclaimed. Then he didn't say anything for several seconds. Brunelle wondered what was happening, but just as he was about to say something, Houser spoke up again. "Okay, where is the email?"

Brunelle peered into the trash can. "It's still there."

"Exactly!" Houser replied. "See?"

Brunelle definitely did not see. He said as much.

Houser frowned slightly, then nodded several times again. "Right. Okay, reach in and take it out. Remember, it never left."

Brunelle did as instructed. "Now what?"

"Now, scratch out the word 'email,'" Houser instructed, "and write something different. Complaint. Write complaint."

"Grandma's in trouble now," Chen mumbled.

Brunelle glared at him, but then did as he was instructed.

"Okay, perfect." Houser pointed at the paper. "Now where is the email?"

Brunelle raised the document slightly. "Right here."

"No!" Houser declared. "That's a brief now. The email is gone."

Brunelle lowered the paper again. "Okay," he drew the word out. "I don't get it."

"That's how computers work," Houser explained. "When

you delete something, it doesn't really go away. You can't access it anymore, but it's still there on the computer's hard drive. It doesn't go away until the computer uses that bit of memory to create a new file, overwriting the old file. Only then is the old file truly destroyed. That's why we can almost always find the things the bad guys think they deleted. They think it's gone, but it's just waiting to be overwritten. And computers today have so much memory that a deleted file may never be overwritten."

"So the emails Grunwald claims he got from the dark web," Brunelle asked, "those are still on the computer somewhere?"

Houser pointed at him. "No!"

"So, that's proof they never existed, right?" Brunelle thought he understood.

Houser pointed at him again. "Also no!"

Brunelle threw his hand up. "The jury is not going to understand this. And I'm not going to be allowed to slam a trash can onto the witness stand."

"The trash can is empty, Dave," Chen explained. "Completely empty. But it should be filled with old papers that say 'email' on them."

"Exactly." Houser crossed his arms triumphantly.

"And what does that mean?" Brunelle asked. "Again, like I'm your average citizen too stupid to get out of jury duty."

"It means he was emptying the trash can before they were overwritten," Houser explained. "Computers don't do that on their own. He installed a program to do it. It deleted every file on the computer every night at midnight."

"Where do you get a program like that?" Brunelle questioned.

"Well, not at some big box store, that's for sure," Houser

answered. "Something like this requires some pretty high-end programming. You'd need to get it from someone who really knows their stuff, and is willing to sell it to you. But you can get anything if you know who to ask."

"And what to ask for," Chen added.

"Would your average plastic surgeon know all that?" Brunelle wondered aloud.

"I wouldn't think so," Houser said. "But this Dr. Grunwald guy sure did."

"And he told his lawyer," Brunelle added. "That's why Milliken knew we wouldn't find anything. He wanted us to look. His guy said he deleted the emails. He thinks we'll think this is proof of that."

"Well, he certainly deleted something," Houser put in. "And we can't say it wasn't threatening emails."

Brunelle frowned at that assessment.

"What else did Milliken say?" Chen asked.

Brunelle considered for a moment. "He said I should talk to Jacoby's wife."

"Are you going to?" Chen questioned.

"No." Brunelle's mouth curved into a grin. "I'm going to talk to Grunwald's."

CHAPTER 12

Brunelle was going to talk to Elizabeth Grunwald, but he wasn't going to do it alone. If for no other reason than that he needed a witness to rebut any claims of impropriety after the interview was complete.

"I was wondering when you'd darken my door again," Carlisle said from her seat behind her desk as Brunelle did indeed darken her office door. "Did you dazzle Marietta Lang at the pretrial? Am I on the case?"

Brunelle grimaced slightly and stepped fully into the office. "A little bit," he offered. "And not quite yet."

Carlisle shook her head. "What about Casey? Did you dazzle her enough to not have to sleep on the couch?"

Brunelle recalled the wager he entered with Casey. "Uh, yeah. That worked out in the end. Just like this will. In the meantime, would you be interested in working on the case in a more unofficial capacity?"

Carlisle raised an eyebrow. "Unofficial capacity?"

"Non-court capacity," Brunelle expounded. "I want to

talk to Grunwald's wife, but I don't want to do it alone."

Carlisle nodded and crossed her arms. "So, you want me to be your investigator. Take notes and be a witness in case she changes her story."

"I was thinking more like in case she files a bar complaint against me," Brunelle replied.

"It would serve you right," Carlisle said. "After abandoning your partner like you did, all because some pretty young thing batted her eyelashes at you."

"She batted them at Matt," Brunelle defended.

"But she is a pretty young thing, apparently," Carlisle said. "You didn't deny that. I'm looking forward to meeting her."

"Aren't you engaged or something?" Brunelle questioned.

"Aren't you?" Carlisle joked. Then, seeing the blood Brunelle felt drain from his face, "Oh my God. Are you and Casey engaged?"

Brunelle took a deep breath and let out a long sigh. "Not exactly. Not yet. It kind of depends on this case."

Carlisle cocked her head and grinned. "What the hell does that mean?"

So, Brunelle explained.

"That is absolutely ridiculous." Carlisle guffawed. "And now you're going to work as hard as you can to prove not just that Grunwald's stated motive is a lie, but that Casey's theory of motive is also wrong. Well, I guess that's one way to motivate you."

Brunelle raised his chin indignantly. "I'm motivated by justice."

Carlisle laughed again and stood up. "Well, luckily I'm motivated by entertainment. No way I'm not there to see how that bet works out, whether I'm officially on the case or not. In the meantime, let's go talk to the defendant's wife. That sounds pretty entertaining too." She pulled a set of keys out of her pocket. "I'll drive."

* * *

Elizabeth Grunwald owned a florist shop in the lobby of the Waxmoore Hotel, a boutique luxury accommodation near the train station in the older part of downtown Seattle. Brunelle didn't suppose it made a lot of money. He also supposed it hadn't mattered given her husband's success. But twenty years in prison would significantly impact his ability to provide her the life Brunelle assumed she was accustomed to.

Or maybe she was a hard-nosed businesswoman.

"Don't give me that shit, Richard," she was yelling into her phone as she paced the entryway of her shop.

Brunelle recognized her from the driver's license photo Chen had pulled for him, along with the rest of her biographical data, like place of employment. She was tall, close to six feet, with long brown hair pulled back tightly into a ponytail. She wore a green merchant's apron over a light blue oxford and black pants. Her shoes were sensible for a day on her feet.

"I don't pay you to try," she continued, "I pay you to do. Do you have any idea how thin our margins are? Do you know how much we rely on repeat business? Do you know the year over year trends for flower delivery? Do you, Richard? No, of course, you don't. So, shut your fucking mouth and do your fucking job. And don't call me again until it's finished."

"So, what's the play?" Carlisle whispered out of the corner of her mouth. "You're getting married and looking for a florist for the wedding. Your wife assigned this one single task to you for the impending nuptials even though you both know you're going to fuck it up. Can she possibly help you not be a complete loser in the eyes of your bride-to-be?"

Brunelle turned to face her fully. "That's pretty specific. Is that what you think is going to happen?"

"When you lose the bet?" Carlisle asked. "No, not really. I don't think Casey will give you even one thing to be in charge of."

Brunelle took a moment then decided to return to the original substance of Carlisle's comments.

"The play is the truth," he said. "We can't lie to people about our role in a case. There's a specific ethical rule on that."

"Funny that there needs to be," Carlisle pointed out.

Brunelle allowed as much with a shrug. "No, we tell her the truth and—"

"Oh, hello," Elizabeth called out to them. "Sorry, I didn't see you earlier. I was, uh, talking with an employee. Are you two interested in some flowers. Do I sense a wedding perhaps?"

"Perhaps," Carlisle answered. "Odds are currently five to three against."

Elizabeth's eyebrows knitted together.

"Please excuse Ms. Carlisle's attempt to break the ice with some humor," Brunelle took over their side of the conversation. "My name is David Brunelle and I'm—"

"You're the man prosecuting my husband!" Elizabeth jabbed a finger at him. "What are you doing here? Bill isn't here. He's at home, no thanks to you. His lawyer told me how you wanted to keep him in jail awaiting trial."

"I did want that," Brunelle admitted. "But we're here at the suggestion of your husband's attorney, Mr. Milliken."

Elizabeth's eyes narrowed. "You are?"

"Essentially," Brunelle qualified with a shrug. "Mr.

Milliken actually suggested we speak with Mrs. Jacoby. He said she would know what her husband was up to. I thought the same logic might apply to you and your husband."

Elizabeth Grunwald crossed her arms and stared at Brunelle for several seconds. "You want me to snitch out my husband?"

"Snitch is a loaded word," Brunelle replied. "We just have a few questions. It might help us understand why Mr. Milliken claims your husband had no choice but to do what he did."

"We don't want to prosecute an innocent man," Carlisle put in, suddenly very serious. "Any information you can provide which helps us understand what really happened that night will be invaluable."

Elizabeth stared at them both until it started to become uncomfortable. Then she stared a bit longer. Brunelle could wait it out. He was a trial lawyer. Enduring awkward pauses was part of the job. Finally, Elizabeth spoke, and when she did, it was with authority.

"The only thing I will tell you, is that I believe my husband when he says he did something someone else told him to do. Now, please leave my store. I need to call Mr. Milliken and tell him you came to question me."

"Ms. Grunwald, please, if—" Carlisle started to protest, but Brunelle grabbed her by the arm.

"Thank you for your time, Ms. Grunwald," he said. "We won't take up any more of it." Then, just to leave her feeling even the slightest bit off balance. "Good luck with Richard."

He and Carlisle crossed the lobby and stepped out onto First Avenue. Clouds were rolling in and the temperature was dropping by the second.

"We should have pressed her more," Carlisle complained.

But Brunelle shook his head. "We'll get our chance when we cross-examine her at trial. She'll have to answer our questions then. She wasn't going to give us much today, but we did learn something."

"That Richard is a shitty employee?" Carlisle quipped.

Brunelle smiled at the joke. But that wasn't his takeaway. "She's used to being in charge. I bet that extends to her marriage. Maybe she was the one who forced Grunwald to pull the trigger."

CHAPTER 13

In preparation for asking Duncan to reconsider his refusal to let Brunelle bring Carlisle on board the Grunwald case, Brunelle thought it might score him some points if he could say he visited the victim in the hospital. He also wanted to pump the doctors for any information about whether and when Jacoby might come out of his coma. What he didn't expect was to run into Veronica Jacoby there. Although he supposed he shouldn't have been surprised.

"Ms. Jacoby," Brunelle blurted out the name upon seeing her sitting bedside in her husband's hospital room.

Veronica looked up from the floor she was staring at blankly. "Oh. Mr. Prosecutor, right?"

"Brunelle," he reminded her. "Dave Brunelle. We met after the arraignment."

"Oh, I remember that," Veronica answered. "I'm just not very good with names."

She seemed notably more subdued than their previous encounter. Sad, even. That made sense. It was just a significant departure from her previous attitude. But if there was one thing Brunelle had learned over years of meeting with the families of murder victims, it was that everyone grieves differently and in their own time.

"What are you doing here?" she asked him. "Are you looking for me? Has there been a development in the case? Is Bill going to plead guilty?"

"I'm afraid the answer is no to all three of those questions," Brunelle replied. "The case is proceeding normally toward trial. The defense attorney has made it clear he won't be pleading his client guilty. And I came here to check in on your husband. I hadn't made it over here yet. To be honest, in most of my cases, I can't visit the victim."

"Why not?" Veronica asked.

Brunelle hesitated. He probably shouldn't have mentioned it. But he had to answer her question. "Uh, well, I do homicides. So, the victims are dead. This case is a little different." Then he remembered to add, "Which is good."

Veronica looked at her husband, still alive but comatose, medical equipment attached to and sticking out of various parts of his body. Brunelle thought he looked peaceful. And way too unconscious to testify. "How is he doing?" he realized he should ask.

Veronica frowned and looked back down at the floor. "The doctors are keeping him alive, but that's all. They said they don't know when he might snap out of his coma." The next words seemed to get stuck in her throat. "Or if he'll ever snap out of it."

"I'm sure it helps to have you here," Brunelle offered.

But Veronica shook her head. "I just came to get his personal effects." She raised a large Ziploc bag with a wallet, a watch, and a few other things in it. Brunelle couldn't make them all out because of the blood smeared on the inside of the bag.

"It's just what was in his pockets," Veronica explained. "His wallet, his Rolex, and some coins. Whatever he had on him when the paramedics brought him here."

"That stuff should probably be in the property room," Brunelle slipped back into job mode. He wasn't great at small talk anyway. "It's evidence."

Veronica looked at the bag again then held it out toward him. "Do you want to take it? He won't be needing these things anytime soon, I'm afraid."

Brunelle hesitated. He wasn't supposed to handle the evidence, just show it off to the jurors once it made its journey from scene, to property room, to crime lab, and finally to the courtroom. Each leg of that journey documented by a law enforcement witness who could testify to the chain of custody.

On the other hand, that chain was probably already broken. And what were the chances he'd need to introduce Harrison Jacoby's wallet or luxury watch at trial? It wasn't an I.D. case, and everybody already knew he and Grunwald were rich.

"Sure," he answered, and stepped over to take the baggie from Veronica. "I'll see to it this gets put into property. You'll get it all back after the trial."

Veronica nodded up at him with large eyes. "When is the trial? Will I have to testify? What about Harry? Can we wait until he's well enough to testify?"

Brunelle looked at the deflated form of Harrison Jacoby and decided not to voice his prognosis as to whether the good doctor would ever sit up again, let alone sit on a witness stand.

"We can't wait if we don't know how long the wait will be," he said instead. "The courts don't really work like that. But yes, you'll need to testify."

"About what?" she questioned. "I wasn't there that night, I swear."

"You wouldn't testify about what happened when your husband was shot," Brunelle responded. "Witnesses can only testify about what they personally observed. There are exceptions, of course. Lawyers made the rules, so there are always exceptions. But I don't want you to talk about that. We have other witnesses who can tell the jury what happened that night. I need you to tell them about what happened before, and what's happened since."

Veronica's lips retracted into a tight frown. "What do you mean, what happened before? Did something else like this happen, and I didn't know about it?"

"No, no." Brunelle waved his hand at that. "I mean, just tell the jury about your husband. About your family. Who he was as a person. They won't get to meet him, so you'll tell them about him instead."

Veronica's expression relaxed. "Well, that doesn't sound too bad."

As he stood there, not entirely unlike a lawyer standing in the center of a courtroom examining a witness sitting on the witness stand, Brunelle recalled Milliken's insinuation at the pretrial conference. *I bet she knows more about this whole sordid affair than she's letting on,* he thought to himself.

"Is there anything I should know now?" he broached the subject. "Was your husband getting along with his partner? Were there new stressors at work or at home? Was he acting like himself?"

Veronica's frown returned, along with lowered eyebrows. "Are you suggesting this is all his fault? Do you think he was doing something that made him deserve what happened to him?"

Brunelle hadn't meant that at all. He was trying to probe her motives, not her husband's. "Oh, no. Of course not. No, I'm sorry if it came across that way. I just meant, did he ever say anything about Dr. Jacoby becoming difficult or even aggressive toward him prior to the shooting? You know, motive stuff."

And he was reminded again of his wager with Casey.

Veronica crossed her arms and pushed back in the chair. "No. Nothing like that. Everything was fine. Everything was like it always had been. Even better. And then Bill just shot him for no reason at all."

Brunelle accepted the answer with a nod.

"You have to make him pay," she added, looking over at what was left of her husband. "You have to make Bill pay for what he did to my Harry."

CHAPTER 14

Brunelle slapped the plastic bag down on the counter.

"I've got some evidence to put into property," he informed the officer on the other side of the window in the basement of Seattle Police Department's main precinct. She was in her fifties, with white hair, large glasses, and an annoyed expression.

"You're not a police officer," she observed.

Brunelle knew she wasn't either. Not commissioned anyway. Commissioned meant she wore a uniform and could carry a gun and handcuffs. Not commissioned meant she wore a gray polo shirt with a Seattle P.D. logo on it, and she carried plastic bags full of bloody personal effects to evidence lockers.

But Brunelle wouldn't begrudge someone doing their job to keep the justice machine running.

"You are correct," he confirmed. He gestured to his own attire, a suit and tie. "I'm a prosecutor. I received this directly from a witness on the Grunwald attempted murder case. I think I probably shouldn't just keep it in my desk drawer."

The man at her window having identified himself as being on the same side if not exactly the same team, the woman's demeanor warmed considerably. "Oh dear. That is no way for a witness to handle evidence. But yes, we'll be happy to take that off your hands. Let me just go grab the forms."

Brunelle relaxed as well, pleased to have cracked the woman's armor and relieved to get the evidence off his hands. He leaned on the counter and turned to gaze absently around his surroundings while he waited.

"Have you read his brief?!"

Carlisle was standing right behind him, a roll of papers in her fist and a look of worry—or worse—on her face.

"It's a really good brief," she added.

Brunelle needed a moment to catch his breath—and slow his heartbeat. "You know I have a heart condition, right? Don't sneak up on me like that."

"Sorry." Carlisle took a step back. She unfurled the document in her hand and offered it to Brunelle. "We got served with Milliken's brief on the duress defense today."

Brunelle accepted the pleading, but cocked his head at Carlisle. "How did you know where I was?"

Carlisle grinned broadly and pointed at Brunelle. "Right. So, first, the courier dropped the brief off with the receptionist. The receptionist gave it to your paralegal. Your paralegal went to give it to you, but you weren't in your office. She came to me because I should be working this fucking case. And then I found you. Ta da!"

Brunelle took a moment. "That doesn't—"

"I called Chen," Carlisle added. "Someone saw you walking into the precinct carrying a bag of blood. That kind of news travels fast."

Brunelle supposed it would. He turned and picked up the baggie. "It's not actually filled with blood. It's filled with things covered in blood."

Carlisle took it from him and held it up to examine the contents. "And what is all this stuff?"

"It's what was in Jacoby's pockets when he got to the hospital." Brunelle explained. "The hospital gave it to his wife and she gave it to me."

"At the hospital?" Carlisle questioned.

"Yeah," Brunelle answered. "I went there to see if I could get the real story on whether he's gonna pull out of it or pass on. She was in his room, though, so I didn't really get the chance."

"Didn't want to suggest to the doc that they unplug him in front of the widow-to-be?"

"I don't want him to die," Brunelle insisted.

Carlisle pointed at the document in his hand. "Read that. You might change your mind. It may be the only way to block that duress defense."

Brunelle frowned at the papers in his hand. He would read it later. It couldn't be that good, he told himself. Unfortunately, he knew he was lying. Before he could say anything more about the duress issue, the property room officer returned with her forms.

"All right then, let's get these inventoried," she announced, pulling on a pair of latex gloves. "I'll extract, you describe."

"Can't you just put the entire bag in as one item?" Brunelle suggested.

The woman took a moment to frown at him. "No. We inventory everything. How else can we know if something is missing?"

Brunelle couldn't disagree. If anything in that bag ever became important, Milliken would savage him over the failure to even write down what was in it. "Good point."

He turned fully back to the property room window. Carlisle stepped up next to him.

"Can I have a pair of gloves too?" she asked.

Brunelle looked askance at her.

"There might be something we want to look at more closely," she explained.

Brunelle shrugged, but didn't argue. He also didn't ask for a pair of gloves.

"Wristwatch. Gold colored. Rolex brand," the property woman voiced her description of the first item she extracted from the bag, before placing into a separate, smaller bag with the word 'PROPERTY' printed on it.

"Car key. Black plastic and silver metal. Lexus brand," was the next description.

Brunelle wondered if the wallet would have a brand. He was pretty sure his didn't. It was just a wallet, from a store.

"Scrap of paper. White with blood stains. Handwriting in blue ink, the words, '1900 Owl Road," the woman said and reached for another individual plastic bag.

"Wait. What?" Carlisle reached out a gloved hand. "Can I see that?"

The property officer made no effort to hand it to her. She also didn't put it in the baggie. "Why?"

Carlisle kept her hand outstretched. "Because I'm one of the prosecutors on the case and I asked to see it."

The woman looked to Brunelle. He nodded. "Those are excellent reasons," he said.

The woman hesitated, sighed loudly, then handed the slip

of paper to Carlisle. Brunelle leaned over to get a good look at it as well. Sure enough, scrawled on the paper in a masculine hand was: '1900 OWL RD'

"Where is Owl Road?" he asked. "I've lived here my whole life, and I don't think I've ever heard of that street."

"Probably Fremont," Carlisle guessed, naming one of the more esoteric neighborhoods in the city. "The better question is, what's at 1900 Owl Road?"

"Can I have that back now?" the property woman asked.

"Hold on," Brunelle answered, pulling his phone from his pocket. "I'm going to take a picture of this."

He did so and Carlisle handed the blood-stained slip of paper back to the property officer. The remainder of the hospital bag's contents were of less interest. Two credit cards, a debit card, and a health insurance card that had also fallen out of the wallet; $112 cash was still inside it. A black pen and a bent paper clip rounded out the items. Property woman finished her inventory and gave them a copy of the property sheet. Brunelle placed it atop the brief Carlisle had delivered to him.

"Now what?" Carlisle asked. "Should we check out 1900 Owl Street?"

"We definitely should," Brunelle agreed, "but first, I want to read Milliken's brief. See what all the fuss is about."

CHAPTER 15

Brunelle read the last sentence and set the brief down on his desk.

"Shit," he hissed to himself.

It really was a good brief. More than good. Thoroughly researched, well-reasoned, persuasive. If Brunelle were the judge, he'd rule in Milliken's favor. That didn't mean the real judge would do so, but it did mean Brunelle couldn't rely on the state of settled law. And if he couldn't win the trial on the law, he was going to need more facts. And more help.

He stood up and headed for Duncan's office. It was time to insist he be allowed to bring Carlisle onto the case. To inform him, not ask him.

Or maybe not.

"Dave!" Duncan stood up from behind his desk as Brunelle entered. "We were just talking about you."

The 'we' in question was Duncan and Marietta Lang, seated opposite Duncan and smiling over her shoulder at him.

"Hello, Dave," she said. "I was just telling Matt about that pretrial conference. I was very impressed by everything that happened that I didn't even know was happening. You really do have a mastery of the position."

"Uh, thanks," Brunelle replied after a moment. "But that's kind of why I wanted to talk to you, Matt. There's even more going on and—"

"Dave." Matt cut him off and raised a warning eyebrow at him. "Take the compliment. I have the utmost confidence in your abilities."

"I do too," Lang added. "In fact, I was wondering if you had the time, and inclination, to educate me."

Brunelle blinked at her. She was wearing a silk blouse and her thick black hair fell loosely onto her shoulders. "About the case, right?"

She laughed. "Of course about the case. What else would it be about?"

"Exactly," Brunelle replied, pointing at her. Then, "Sure, I can do that."

Lang pushed herself out of her chair. "How about right now? Matt and I were just finishing our meeting."

"Go ahead, Dave." Duncan stood up as well and waved them toward the door. "We can talk after you've met with Marietta. That is, if you still want to."

Brunelle was certain he would still want to. Lang sauntered past him in a red pencil skirt and heels. But he was less certain than he had been when he'd walked into Duncan's office.

He turned and followed Lang to his office, being sure to keep his gaze firmly on the carpet in front of him. When he reached his office, Lang was already inside, seated in one of the guest chairs on the opposite side of his desk from where he quickly sat down.

"So, uh, what did you want to know about?" Brunelle asked.

Lang leaned forward. "Anything. Everything."

Brunelle nodded. He didn't understand why Lang was suddenly acting so... friendly. He wasn't even sure she really was. He had a history of misinterpreting that sort of thing. He thought he was past that sort of thing. But maybe he was wrong.

"Maybe you can explain all of that stuff about the defense the attorney was talking about," Lang suggested. "That seemed to be important, but you two didn't really get into details. It was like you each knew what the other was going to say, so you didn't bother saying it."

"Duress," Brunelle labeled it.

"Yes!" Lang pointed a perfectly manicured, blood red nail at him. "Duress. What is duress?"

So, Brunelle explained it, to what he thought were a few too many 'ah's and oh's.' And definitely too many giggles. There should have been zero giggles.

"So, duress is being forced to do something you don't really want to do?" Lang summarized. "But maybe you sort of do want to do it or else you wouldn't."

"I suppose that's not a terrible definition," Brunelle agreed.

"Sounds like it could be fun," Lang smiled at him, "with the right person."

"Sure," was all Brunelle could think to say.

"It seemed like you really understood that." She tucked a strand of hair behind her ear. "Have you ever done something you shouldn't have done? You told yourself someone made you do it? But really, deep down, you wanted to?"

A rush of memories, or at least a few of the best, flooded

his mind. His pulse quickened, to no good for that heart condition. Finally, he nodded. "Yes."

Lang smiled broadly. "I thought so, Dave." She stood up. "I think I've learned what I wanted to. For now. I'm looking forward to learning more soon."

She took her leave then. Brunelle could only sit at his desk and watch after her as she slipped through his doorway. As she did so, Carlisle became visible through it, standing in the hallway, frowning and shaking her head. He wondered how long she'd been standing there.

"What the hell was that?" she demanded as she stormed into his office.

"What the hell was what?" Brunelle defended. "She just had some questions about the case."

"So, you were giving her some private tutoring, huh?" Carlisle asked in a suggestive tone.

Brunelle crossed his arms. "It wasn't like that."

"Oh no?" Carlisle challenged. "Have you gotten me on the case yet? Wasn't that the plan? Or do you need to take Marietta out for dinner first?"

"I just went to talk to Duncan about it," Brunelle answered, "but didn't get the chance because somehow I ended up explaining duress to Lang."

"Somehow? Ha!" Carlisle scoffed. "I think we both know how."

Brunelle took a moment. "You seem really upset."

"Of course I'm upset!" Carlisle threw her hands up.

"Why?" Brunelle asked. "Because I haven't gotten you assigned to the case yet?"

"No, you dumbass," Carlisle turned toward the door. "Because what if that had been Casey standing in the hallway watching all of that instead of me?"

Brunelle had no words.

"Call me if I'm ever officially on the case," Carlisle said before she exited, "but don't bother me again until then. You want to do this on your own, fine. But one of these days, Dave, you really will be all on your own. And you won't have anyone to blame but yourself."

CHAPTER 16

Brunelle arrived home from work feeling a mix of emotions he realized he hadn't endured for some time. Which led him to feel additional feelings that he didn't particularly like either. And she was cooking dinner already.

"Hey, I'm home," he called out. He set his briefcase by the door and kicked off his shoes. Whatever she was cooking smelled delicious. He should be sure to cook their next dinner.

"Hello, handsome," Casey called back to him. "Dinner is halfway done. Can you pour us a couple of drinks?"

He definitely could, but first he walked up behind his girlfriend and wrapped his arms around her. He hugged her tight and buried his face into her neck.

"Whoa, tiger." Casey giggled and reached back to grab the back of his head. "What brought this on? Tough day at work?"

"I don't want to think about my day at work," Brunelle said from beneath her hair. "I just want to think about you."

"Ok, but dinner is going to burn if you don't slow down,"

Casey laughed again.

"Turn the burners off," Brunelle suggested, pulling her closer to him. "We can pick up where we left off."

"You don't cook a lot, do you?" Casey responded. "It doesn't work that way. Not this meal."

"I'll cook something else, then," Brunelle offered. "Or we get takeout. Or we starve."

"Starve?" Casey spun around to hold each other face-to-face. "That's not a great sales pitch."

"We'll nourish ourselves from our love," Brunelle stepped backward toward the bedroom.

"Gross," Casey replied with a laugh. "And inadequate. But I know you were going for romantic, so I'll give you points for it."

"I'll give you more than points," Brunelle growled and kissed her deeply.

Casey kissed back just as hard, then pulled away long enough to turn off the burners.

"All right, lover boy, you win," she fell back into his arms. "Make it worth it."

Brunelle had every intention of doing so.

* * *

Brunelle returned from the bathroom and fell into bed, still naked. Casey, also still nude, laid her head on his chest and ran a finger down his stomach.

"That was definitely worth it," she purred.

Brunelle squeezed her tightly.

"Whatever happened at work today," Casey added, "make sure it happens again."

Brunelle frowned, but Casey couldn't see it. That was the last thing he wanted. "How about I make sure what happened tonight at home happens again?"

"Mmm." Casey rubbed her hand across his chest. "I'll take that."

Brunelle didn't reply, lost again in the thoughts he had tried to drown.

"You okay?" Casey asked, tipped her head to look up at him.

He made sure to smile. "Of course." And he gave her another hug. "You know me. I can't stop thinking about work for long. So, what do you want for dinner?"

"I think I can probably salvage what I was working on when you got home," Casey offered.

She started to push herself off his chest. Brunelle felt assaulted by the sudden absence of her. He pulled her back onto him.

"Never mind," he said. "Let's lie here a bit more. Dinner can wait a few more minutes. And work can wait until tomorrow."

Casey smiled again and nuzzled her head back down onto his chest. She didn't say anything else, and Brunelle knew to do the same.

CHAPTER 17

The next morning, Brunelle was feeling pretty good about himself. He and Casey had finished preparing dinner together, salvaging what they could from her original plans and adding what they could find in the cupboards and refrigerator to assemble an appetizing meal. He picked out one of his favorite ties, stopped on the way to pick up a coffee, and made it to his desk on time and in good spirits.

Then he saw Milliken's brief still lying atop his desk. He set down his coffee and picked up the brief. The worst part of Milliken's brief wasn't that it was so good; it was that Brunelle would have to write a response. Setting aside the question of whether he could muster an argument persuasive enough to neutralize Milliken's key points, Brunelle just didn't really enjoy writing briefs. He was a trial lawyer. He loved the electricity of a full courtroom and the sound of his own voice commanding the proceedings. There was no way to replicate that sitting behind a keyboard and making sure the case citations were formatted properly.

Which left Brunelle with a choice. Do something boring, or push it off and do something exciting. His response brief wasn't due for six more days anyway. All the time in the world. The choice was clear. Especially if the something exciting might lead to something useful for the something boring.

He picked up his phone and dialed Chen's number. If he was in danger of losing the motion on the law, he needed better facts. The sort of facts he might find at 1900 Owl Road, wherever that was.

But Chen didn't cooperate.

"You've reached the desk of Detective Chen with the Seattle Police Department. Please leave a message and I will return your call when I am able. Thank you."

Brunelle frowned at the development, but left a message anyway.

"Larry. It's Dave. I've got a new lead on the Grunwald case. Thought we could try to check it out together. Give me a call."

He ended the call and sighed.

Guess I'll work on that response after all, he said to himself. No one else was going to do it for him. Not until he got Carlisle on the case. But he wasn't quite ready to wade back into whatever it was that had happened the previous day. He was well aware that most of the time, the best way out was through. But there was something to be said for letting things solidify before trying to break through them again.

He closed his office door, then trudged around his desk and dropped himself into his chair. He pulled the brief over to him and turned on his computer. While he waited for the screen to light up, he took another drink of his coffee. It had turned bitter.

* * *

The three main points of Milliken's brief were that traditionally duress was available for any crime, that the Legislature drafted the duress statute to exclude murder, and they did not choose to also exclude attempted murder. Therefore, the courts were wrong to extend the statutory exclusion beyond what the Legislature had chosen to do. Fair reasoning.

Brunelle needed to respond to all three in turn, but again, he was a trial lawyer, not a legal historian. Generally speaking, he didn't need to know the history of a law to be able to enforce it. Especially since his trade was murder cases. Murder had been illegal pretty much since people starting writing down laws. As a result, the drafting was slow and arduous, fueled by too much coffee and not enough lunch. Eventually, Brunelle had a skeleton of a first draft completed. By then, it was after 5:00 p.m. Chen had never called back.

Brunelle stood up to stretch his back and consider his options. He could try Chen again and seem desperate. He could ask Carlisle, despite her directive not to contact her until she was officially on the case. He could see if Casey was up for a strange, mid-week date night adventure. Or he could do what he was going to do anyway: go find Owl Road on his own and see what he could see.

He turned off what needed to be turned off, picked up what needed to be picked up, and made his way down the elevator and up the street to where the government workers had to park because the hundred-year-old courthouse didn't have underground parking as had become mandated for all new office towers. It was just as well though. A light drizzle danced over his features and seemed to wash off the dullness brought on by a day of reading and writing. He was ready for some action. Or at least, he thought he was.

Step one was determining whether there was an Owl Road in Seattle. A quick search on his phone confirmed there was not. That was hardly surprising. Seattle used a grid system for most of its street names. Avenues ran north-south and streets ran east-west. Starting at First Avenue and Main Street in the old downtown south of the commercial districts, the streets north of Main and east of First Avenue were Northeast First Street, Northeast Second Street, and so on, all the way out of Seattle up to the county line and NE 205th Street. North of Main and west of First Avenue were NW First Street, etc., with the southern streets extending to the other end of the county and SW 368th Street. There was less land to the west so the Avenues ran from 65th Avenue SW in West Seattle to 477th Avenue SE just past Riverbend in the foothills of the Cascade Mountains, where the numbering systems switched to National Forest roads. The main exceptions to the grid system were the street names in the downtown core, none of which were Owl, and the neighborhoods to the northwest of downtown that were laid out prior to some government bean-counter like Marietta Lang deciding to take all the fun out of naming streets. Neighborhoods like Magnolia, Ballard, and Carlisle's suggestion: Fremont.

"Fremont it is," Brunelle announced to himself, as he put his car into gear. "Home of a thousand and one microbreweries, a twenty-four-hour flea market, and a giant troll sculpture under a bridge."

If there was a neighborhood in the city that was hiding a secret Owl Road, it was Fremont.

"Bunch of hippies," Brunelle muttered to himself, not without some begrudging admiration.

CHAPTER 18

Hippies and techies, Brunelle amended as he crossed the Fremont Bridge and spied the latest regional headquarters of Google, or Amazon, or Meta, jutting out into the canal that led from Lake Washington to Elliott Bay. Prime waterfront property converted from, most likely, a fish cannery to the latest open-concept, hotel-model, dynaoffice. That tech mantra, 'Move fast and break things,' seemed to break a lot more outside of tech than it ever did inside, in Brunelle's humble opinion. That his opinion was shared by others was confirmed as he reached the other side of the bridge and spied a sticker on a power box that read, 'Keep Fremont Weird.'

The persistent drizzle was darkening the sky in advance of sunset. Brunelle decided to park at the center of the neighborhood, on Fremont Avenue itself, and explore the neighborhood by walking in ever-increasing circles, a stilted spiral of exploration looking for anything the locals might call Owl Road, even if none of the search engines of the aforementioned tech giants did so.

He squeezed into a parking space near 36th Street, a few blocks from the water, and began his quest. The first stop was Hidden Gems Antique Shop. He had joked about the number of microbreweries in Fremont, but there were probably even more antique shops, the majority of whose 'antiques' dated from the 1960s and 70s. Upon entering, Brunelle spied a metal lunchbox he was pretty sure he'd had when he was in Mrs. Retelle's third grade class.

"Can I help you find anything?" a woman behind a countertop full of frosted glass candle cylinders asked. She had gray hair pulled back carelessly in what might have been, with more effort, a ponytail. A flannel jacket-shirt covered a flannel henley. Large glasses covered a face completely bereft of makeup. Her smile was genuine and warm.

"Actually, yes." Brunelle stepped over to the counter. "I'm trying to find Owl Road. Is that nearby?"

The woman tipped her head slightly. "Owl Road?"

"Owl Street?" Brunelle allowed. "Owl Avenue? Anything like that?"

There was no guarantee Jacoby hadn't gotten the exact designation of the thoroughfare wrong. The main thing seemed to be 'Owl.'

"There's no Owl Road around here," the woman answered. "I know there's an Osprey Street in Oak Harbor. I don't suppose that helps much."

Oak Harbor was 50 miles and two counties away.

"No, not really," Brunelle agreed. He examined a faux pearl necklace hanging from a wooden rack, wondering whether Casey might like it. Probably not. "Maybe one of the alleyways around here? Something people just call Owl Road unofficially because, oh I don't know, somebody found a dead owl there once or something."

The woman frowned at him. "That's kind of dark."

Brunelle supposed it was. He admitted as much.

The woman took a longer, more appraising glance at the man in her shop. "That's a nice suit. You don't see a lot of people wearing suits anymore. Not in Fremont anyway. Even those new techies wear button-up shirts but no ties. What line of work are you in? And is that why you're poking around asking about dead owls?"

Brunelle smiled at the woman. He liked anyone who was blunt enough to ask why he was dressed like it was twenty years earlier.

"I'm a lawyer," he fairly admitted. "A prosecutor."

Everyone hated lawyers. Whether they liked prosecutors depended on where they generally stood regarding committing crimes. A lot had changed in those twenty-plus years since Brunelle first started wearing a suit to the courthouse. Possession of cannabis used to carry a mandatory day in jail; now there were pot shops in every neighborhood. Fremont probably had two. People who traveled in circles that committed those sorts of victimless crimes tended not to be fond of middle-aged men in suits who paid their rent by putting their friends in cages. But no one—almost no one—condoned murder.

"Homicide prosecutor," he added. "I'm trying to track down a lead on my latest case."

"Homicide?" The woman's eyes widened appropriately. "Did someone get murdered in Fremont? I feel like I would have heard about that. We're a tight-knit community. At least we're trying to stay that way."

"Gentrification comes for us all," Brunelle quipped. He would have told her he somehow ended up living in the suburbs, but if there was a person the average Seattleite disliked more than a prosecutor it would be a someone from Bellevue.

"Isn't that the truth?" the woman agreed.

"But no," Brunelle answered the question. "There was no murder in Fremont. At least, that's not my case. There was an attempted murder on First Hill, and the victim had a slip of paper in his wallet with an address on Owl Road. There's no Owl Road in Seattle, or anywhere in King County that I could find. But I thought if there was some weird backstreet that the locals secretly called Owl Road, it would be in Fremont."

The woman nodded along to the explanation. "And you're trying to put the attempted murderer in jail?"

Brunelle nodded, but he was still going to soft peddle his law enforcement role. The woman seemed to appreciate him, but he was still in the neighborhood that had had a statue of Lenin and celebrated the winter solstice with an annual parade proudly featuring naked bicyclists.

"I like to think of it as trying to hold him responsible for his actions," he explained. "I get the jury to confirm he did it, and then the Legislature and the judge decide what the punishment should be."

"Did he do it?" she asked. That was always the question.

"Definitely," Brunelle answered. "He confessed to it. He's just claiming he had to do it."

"Why?"

Brunelle grinned and shrugged. "That's why I'm looking for Owl Road. I think whatever I find there will help me answer that question."

"What happens if he really did have to do it?" she asked, becoming notably interested in the fate of a man she'd never even heard of prior to their conversation.

"Then the jury will acquit him," Brunelle answered. "He'll walk away a free man."

The woman leaned forward and tapped a finger on her lips. "And this information on Owl Road, wherever that is, what if it proves he's innocent? Will you cover it up?"

"Oh no, of course not," Brunelle answered. "I'll turn it over to the defense attorney. I have to. That's part of my job. And if I'm convinced he's innocent, I'll dismiss the case. It won't even go to a jury."

The woman stood up again and threw another appraising glance at him. "Really?"

"Really."

She crossed her arms. "Have you ever done that before? Have you ever dismissed a murder case because you found new evidence that proved the person was innocent?"

Brunelle wasn't sure whether he was proud of his answer, but he supposed he should be. "Yes."

The woman nodded several times, then pointed toward the exit. "Go to The Purple Pig. It's a tavern around the corner on Thirty-Seventh. Tim is one of the bartenders there. If anyone knows about some secret street in Fremont, it's Tim. Tell him Brenda sent you."

Brunelle smiled. "Thanks, Brenda." He picked up that necklace after all. "And I'd like to buy this."

* * *

The Purple Pig had one of those entrances that was on the corner of the building. A heavy wooden door under a hanging sign with a carving of a pig. Years of rain had worn most of the paint off of the sign, but Brunelle could imagine the pig had been bright purple at one time. He pulled the door open and stepped inside the pub.

The smell of fried food and beer reminded him he hadn't eaten dinner yet. He supposed he could pump Tim for information over a burger and fries. And a Manhattan. Definitely a Manhattan. Brunelle eschewed the well-lit room full of tables near the windows for the dimly lit but fully stocked bar on the opposite side of the establishment. Whatever dinner rush they might experience on weekday evenings didn't seem to have started yet, so Brunelle was able to secure a seat at the bar two stools away from the only other occupant, one of those techies with his khaki pants, blue button-up shirt, and no tie. He was staring at his phone and didn't look up when the bartender set down a pint of undoubtedly local ale in front of him.

Brunelle left his own phone in his pants pocket and picked up a cocktail menu sitting on the bar a half-seat or so to his right.

"See something you like?" The bartender stepped over to him. He was a large man, wearing a striped shirt with the cuffs rolled up and a black vest buttoned up against a barrel chest. Tattoos covered what Brunelle could see of his arms and a well-trimmed red beard extended several inches below his jawline.

Brunelle hadn't even had time to check out whatever their house variations on the usual cocktails were. Adding orange liqueur to the Old Fashioned, or honey and rosemary to the Negroni. It was always something. Something he wasn't interested in.

"Can I just get a classic Manhattan?" He nodded toward the bottles behind the bartender.

"Well whiskey okay?" the bartender asked.

"Well is fine," Brunelle answered. "I'm not fancy."

The bartender smirked at his outfit. "Fancy suit." Then, stepping away again. "One Manhattan, coming up."

Brunelle turned around and surveyed the tavern while he

waited for his drink. In addition to the phone-addicted techie near him, there were several groups of people scattered across the dining area. The windows on the other side of the room offered a view mostly of the stores across the street, but suggested the waterway beyond by the lack of trees in the distance and the bridge just visible to the right. Everyone seemed happy enough, and there was nothing particularly interesting about anyone there. And not an owl in sight.

"Here's your Manhattan, sir." The bartender returned with his drink quicker than Brunelle had expected. Then again, it was still slow, especially at the bar.

"Thanks." Brunelle spun back and pulled the amber beverage toward him. "Your name doesn't happen to be Tim, does it?"

The bartender stood up just a bit taller and tipped his head ever so slightly. Brunelle could relate. It was never comfortable when someone you didn't know seemed to know you. In his line of work, a 'You don't remember me, do you?' could definitely be followed with a 'You sent me to prison.' Brunelle supposed there was some equally uncomfortable situation for bartenders. Probably several.

"Yes," he admitted after a moment. "Who's asking?"

"I'll start with who's telling," Brunelle replied. "Brenda at the antique shop around the corner."

Tim visibly relaxed.

"She said I should talk to you," Brunelle continued. "She said if anyone knew what I was looking for, it would be you."

Tim nodded. "Okay. Brenda is good people. What can I help you with?"

Brunelle took a swig of his drink. "I'm looking for Owl Road. And yes, I know that sounds like a bad folk song."

"Owl Road?" Tim repeated, rolling the idea around his mouth before kicking it up to his brain. "There's no Owl Road in Fremont."

So, Brunelle told him the whole story. The doctors, the shooting, the wallet, the slip of paper, everything. If Brenda trusted Tim, Brunelle decided he could too. He ignored the obvious fact that he had no idea if he could trust Brenda.

When he finished, Tim crossed his arms and clicked his tongue. "I don't think you're going to find your Owl Road here, sir. Or Owl anything. Fremont is filled with old hippies and young hipsters. Gray hair and wrinkles are signs of longevity against a world that wants everyone to consume and conform. No one around here is getting plastic surgery." He stole the quickest of glances at Brunelle's bar mate. "Well, almost no one."

Brunelle looked over at the man to his right as well. He hadn't taken a good look before, but he did so then. The man was young, younger than Brunelle anyway. Probably still in his twenties. He had short brown hair, thick glasses, and a struggling beard that was losing the struggle. He was still staring at his phone, but to Brunelle's considerable surprise, he finally said something, and to Brunelle.

"He's mostly correct, but he's not entirely correct."

"I beg your pardon?" Brunelle asked.

Tim rolled his eyes and stepped away. An important part of bartending was staying out of patrons' conversations.

"I said," the techie finally set down his phone and turned to Brunelle, "that the bartender is mostly correct, but not entirely correct."

"I heard what you said," Brunelle replied. "I just wasn't sure what you meant. You think there are people in Fremont who have had cosmetic procedures done?"

The man just blinked at him. Tim took a moment to glance over and surrender an unprofessional shake of the head. Brunelle, for his part, decided to check his judgment. Anyone who had information, or even just an opinion, about his investigation was worth engaging with.

He extended a hand. "I'm Dave."

The man just looked at it. "Okay."

Brunelle took a beat, then retracted his hand. "Aren't you going to tell me your name?"

The man thought for a moment, then shook his head. "No. I don't know you, and I don't really want to know you. I just wanted you to know that the bartender is wrong."

"You said he was mostly right," Brunelle reminded the man.

"Mostly right is still wrong," the man said. He stood up and pulled a hundred-dollar bill from his wallet to set on the bar. "Good luck with your hunt, Dave, but I don't wish you success."

"That seems contradictory," Brunelle remarked, hoping to goad the man into further conversation.

"Does it?" the man replied. "I don't think so."

And with that, the man departed and stepped out into the rain that had picked up while Brunelle was inside. It seemed to have no effect on the man as he walked past the windows and out of sight.

"That guy's an asshole," Tim stepped back over to say. "Comes in almost every night, never talks to anyone." He picked up the C-note. "But he tips good."

Brunelle looked again out the window where the man had disappeared. "He talked to me."

CHAPTER 19

Brunelle spent the rest of the week revising his response and wondering about the strange man at The Purple Pig. By Friday afternoon, he was increasingly satisfied with his brief and increasingly unsatisfied with his interaction with the man at the bar. He knew enough to know there was more going on in the case than he knew. In his experience, the best way to unravel knots was to bounce ideas off another person equally invested in solving the problem. A coworker. Coconspirator. Co-counsel.

It was time to talk to Duncan again. But again, Marietta Lang got in the way.

"Oh!" Lang called out when she saw Brunelle walk into the small waiting area outside Duncan's office. She stood up and smoothed out her outfit. A green bodycon dress under a sharp black blazer. Her hair was combed straight back from her face again, parted crisply down the middle and falling like a waterfall down her back. "I'm so happy to see you again."

Brunelle offered a curt, "Hello," then turned his attention to Duncan's administrative assistant, Jennifer Tan. "Will Matt have a few minutes for me before the end of the day?"

"I have an appointment with him in five minutes," Lang spoke up again. "We could do it together."

Brunelle suppressed a wince. "It's kind of a lawyer thing. You wouldn't be interested."

Lang, of course, would have been extremely interested. She was the one thing that had stood in the way of Brunelle and his standard operating procedure.

"Try me," she replied. "I'm very interested in you, Dave."

Jennifer raised her eyebrows at Brunelle. He tried not to react. "Does Matt have time for me?" he repeated his inquiry.

Jennifer checked her computer monitor and frowned. "He might be willing to squeeze you in at the end of the day. He's booked until five-thirty, then he needs to get across town by six for a fundraiser."

"Damn," Brunelle hissed.

"In fact, he's already running behind." Jennifer looked up at Lang. "He probably won't be ready for you, Ms. Lang, for another twenty minutes or so."

Instead of seeming disappointed, Lang's face lit up. "Oh good! Dave and I can catch up on his case. There's a big hearing coming up, if I recall correctly. And I always recall correctly."

Brunelle sighed. "Ask Matt to stay late for me. I'll be back at five-thirty. I don't have any plans tonight."

"Don't be so sure," Lang interjected, walking by Brunelle and stroking a finger under his chin. "Let's go to your office. I have a proposition for you."

When Brunelle didn't respond, frozen in place, she insisted, "Professional, of course."

Brunelle looked at Jennifer again. She clearly didn't believe it either.

"It looks like you really do need to talk to Matt," Jennifer said. I'll make sure he stays for you."

"Thanks, Jennifer," Brunelle responded. He looked down the hallway. Lang was already halfway to his office. She sure knew how to look good.

Jennifer wished him, "Good luck."

Brunelle thanked her again then made his way back to his office. Lang was already inside, sitting in his chair, high heels on his desk.

"There you are," she pulled her feet back onto the ground. "Nice chair, by the way. Does everyone get these, or just the top prosecutors like you?"

She made enough room for Brunelle to claim his chair, but he would have to brush by her to do so. He opted to sit in one of his own guest chairs instead.

"I just get whatever they give me," he answered. "That's how government works. I don't have clients I need to impress."

Lang hung a lopsided half frown on her perfectly colored lips and dropped back into his chair. He noted it would smell like her after she left.

"Well, you're impressive nonetheless, Dave. I've been asking around about you."

"You have?" Brunelle asked before realizing he probably shouldn't have.

"Oh, yes," Lang answered. "Everyone agreed you're an excellent prosecutor. One of the best in the office. That's why you get big cases like the Grunwald case."

"Well, that's nice to hear, I suppose," he said.

"Opinions were more divided on your personal life," Lang continued.

"My personal life?" Brunelle bristled. "People shouldn't

have opinions on my personal life."

Lang laughed, showing off bright white teeth and a smooth throat. "Oh come now, Dave. Everyone has opinions about everyone else. Especially people who've worked together for years. I learned a lot about you, actually."

"Okay." Brunelle tried to be as noncommittal as possible.

"For instance," Lang continued, "you're not married, not even engaged."

Brunelle raised a finger to protest but hesitated at the truth of the statement.

"You tend to date within your profession," Lang continued. "I've heard stories of failed romances with defense attorneys, medical examiners, even cops."

"I wouldn't say 'failed,'" Brunelle started to protest, but Lang walked around the desk and continued.

"Have you ever heard that phrase, 'Don't shit where you eat'?"

Brunelle had, of course. He thought it was weirdly crass for the thought it was trying to convey.

"You should try dating outside of the criminal justice system." Lang sat on the desk directly in front of him and crossed her stockinged legs. A sort of fishnet with a flower pattern.

"I'm in a relationship right now," Brunelle informed her. "With one of those cops you mentioned, in fact."

"Oh, I know." Lang nodded. "And I know it's already lasted longer than any of the others everyone here has watched you burn through. So, that either means it's something special, or it's already past its expiration date. So, wanna have dinner with me tonight?"

Brunelle leaned back in his chair and shook his head. "That is not a good idea."

Lang shrugged. "I guess that depends on what the goal is. It could really help out that career of yours you seem so married to, if you'll excuse the expression."

Brunelle cocked his head at her.

"My report will be really important to how things are done here moving forward," Lang expounded. "Real make or break time, you know. More funding, or severe budget cuts? How many people would lose their jobs if your budget was cut by, say, thirty percent? How would that impact your ability to do what you love? Would more criminals get away with their crimes? What if the budget increased? How many more prosecutors could you hire? How much more justice could you do? That's what you care about, right? Justice?"

Brunelle nodded stiffly. "I care about justice."

"Great!" Lang clapped her hands and leaned forward, pushing her curves toward him. "Look, you're going to eat tonight anyway, right? Why not share a meal with me? One dinner. Am I so bad to look at?"

Marietta Lang was definitely not bad to look at. That was the problem with even one dinner.

Brunelle stood up abruptly and extended an arm toward her. She started to lean into it, but Brunelle reached past her and grabbed the latest draft of his response brief that was lying behind her.

"I have to go," he announced. "Justice stuff."

Lang stood up and flipped her hair down her back again. "You didn't say no. Don't leave a girl hanging."

"I've left one hanging too long already," Brunelle replied from the doorway. "And no."

He left Lang in his office and marched directly to Carlisle's. She was still there, of course. Gwen Carlisle didn't leave early, even on a Friday afternoon.

"Here." Brunelle tossed the brief on her desk. "Read this."

Carlisle picked it up long enough to confirm the case caption then dropped it again. "I told you, I'm not working on this until I'm officially on the case."

"You're on the case," Brunelle replied. "Officially."

"Duncan okayed that?" Carlisle snatched the brief up again.

"I okayed it," Brunelle answered. "I need you on the case."

Carlisle leaned back and grinned. "You need a talented and aggressive co-counsel?"

Brunelle shook his head. "I need a witness."

CHAPTER 20

The courtroom was packed for the hearing on Milliken's motion to allow the duress defense. They had drawn Judge Andrew Parmenter. It was universally agreed among the lawyers that practiced in front of him that Parmenter was the smartest judge on the King County bench. It was almost as agreed that he was the smartest judge in the state. Even smarter than those with greater ambition who had ascended to the appellate courts. In fact, his decision not to seek higher office was often cited as proof of his superior intellect. Arguing in front of Judge Parmenter already felt like arguing in front of the State Supreme Court. He didn't need eight lesser minds muddying up his rulings.

All of that was bad news for Brunelle and Carlisle. A judge of average intellect was unlikely to do anything other than follow the existing law. That was what trial court judges were supposed to do. Appellate court judges crafted the rules. Trial court judges just applied them. With a judge like Linda Ketelbaum or Michael Jakobsen, the hearing would consist of the judge challenging Milliken on why they should deviate from existing law, allowing Milliken to make his record, then denying the motion and encouraging him to appeal to the Court of Appeals. With Parmenter, they were already there, in spirit.

"Full house," Carlisle observed. She nodded toward the front row. "Your new girlfriend is even here."

Marietta Lang was scanning the courtroom and spied Brunelle looking at her. She smiled and waved. Burgundy fingernails matched her lips and jacket.

"Wave back," Carlisle encouraged out of the corner of her mouth. "She can still cut our budget in half."

Brunelle summoned a weak smile and minimal wave.

Milliken was already at the defense table, of course, with his client seated next to him. Several cameras lined the back wall, and the gallery in between was filled with the professionally and personally curious. The back rows held the junior prosecutors and defense attorneys who normally haunted the courthouse and didn't want to pass up an opportunity to see two heavyweights slug it out in front of the Smartest Judge in the Room. The front row was reserved, wedding-like, for the families. Behind the defense table sat Elizabeth Grunwald. Behind the prosecution table sat Veronica Jacoby—and Marietta Lang.

Brunelle and Carlisle made their way forward to a smattering of well wishes from the prosecutors in the crowd. The defense attorneys in attendance offered no more than sneers and scowls, with the exception of Jessica Edwards, who was seated directly behind Mrs. Grunwald.

"Interesting issue," she said when Brunelle noticed her. "This could have a pretty significant fallout for other cases."

"Only if we lose," Brunelle replied.

Edwards smiled. "Exactly. That's what I'm hoping for."

Brunelle only nodded in reply and he and Carlisle

stepped forward to their table. Milliken had been feigning focus on the papers in front of him. He looked up at Brunelle's arrival, likely to offer no more than an acknowledging nod, but his stoic expression lit up at the sight of Carlisle.

"You've brought reinforcements?" he goaded. "I'm flattered."

"Don't be," Brunelle responded. "I'll do whatever it takes to hold your client responsible for what he did."

Milliken's smug grin faded slightly. "What he did was legally excusable. At least, it will be after this hearing."

Brunelle wasn't one for trash talk. There would be more than enough talking once Parmenter took the bench in a few short minutes. It was 8:57 a.m. and Parmenter was as punctual as he was intelligent.

"Dave!" Lang's voice came from behind in a raspy half-whisper. "Dave!"

Brunelle sighed and turned around. Lang was standing up and leaning over the half-wall that separated the gallery from the front of the courtroom.

"I wanted to say congratulations," Lang said in a normal tone.

Brunelle lowered his eyebrows. "I haven't won the hearing yet."

"No, no." Lang waved her hand at him. "Not the hearing. Your engagement."

Carlisle looked at Brunelle with the same puzzled expression Brunelle knew he was showing Lang. "Engagement?"

"When you left your office last Friday," Lang explained, "you said you have a girl you'd left hanging too long. I assumed you meant your girlfriend. Did you not propose to her this weekend?"

Brunelle blinked at Lang for several moments. "No," he fairly admitted.

"Oh." Lang smiled. "Good."

She sat down again. "Good luck. We'll talk later."

Brunelle wished that weren't true. He sat down at his table, Carlisle joining him.

"That's going to be a problem for you," she opined in a whisper.

Brunelle agreed but he didn't want to talk about it just then. He needed to regain his focus. The hearing was about to start.

"All rise!" called the bailiff. "The King County Superior Court is now in session, The Honorable Andrew Parmenter presiding."

Parmenter emerged from his chambers and took his seat on the bench above the crowded courtroom.

"Please be seated," he instructed.

He was in his sixties, ready for retirement but uninterested in it. Wisps of gray hair arched over his ears and framed a bald head dotted with a collection of age spots of varying darknesses. Black-framed glasses sat halfway down his nose. He had a thick white mustache but no beard. A thin neck disappeared into the flowing black robe that concealed his body, to no detriment to his command of the room. It was his mind that had earned the respect of those who appeared before him.

"Are the parties ready on the matter of *The State of Washington versus William Grunwald*?"

Brunelle stood to reply first. The prosecution always replied first, and the lawyers always stood to address the judge. "The State is ready, Your Honor. David Brunelle and Gwen Carlisle, on behalf of the State of Washington."

Milliken stood next, even as Brunelle returned to his seat. "Derek Milliken, appearing on behalf of the defendant, Dr. William Grunwald. The defense is ready as well."

"Good, good." Parmenter nodded upon completion of the commencement protocols. "I see we have many interested observers with us this morning. Excellent. I, too, am interested to hear the arguments of counsel on this intriguing and important question of law."

Brunelle stifled a sigh. Important was fine, but he didn't want it to be intriguing. He wanted it to be boring. Settled. It was supposed to be settled.

"This is the defendant's motion." Parmenter opened a hand toward the defense table. "Whenever you are ready, Mr. Milliken."

Milliken, who had remained standing, nodded up to the judge. "Thank you, Your Honor. May it please the Court. I have the honor today to represent an innocent man in his noble quest to prove his innocence. I think it is worth noting that, although our criminal justice rests, and rightly so, on the bedrock principles of the presumption of innocence, proof beyond a reasonable doubt, and the right to remain silent, Dr. Grunwald has chosen to seek shelter in none of these sacrosanct doctrines. Rather, he wishes to tell his story, because his story is what will prove, beyond any doubt, reasonable or otherwise, that his actions, while tragic and regrettable, were nevertheless legally justified under the centuries-old doctrine of duress."

That was a lot of words, Brunelle thought to himself. The trial, if they ever got to it, was going to take forever.

"But as old as that doctrine is," Milliken continued, "there is one even older and even more important. Indeed, it is the fundamental principle upon which all of our criminal law stands.

One simple in its formulation, yet invaluable in its prescription."

Milliken took a dramatic pause, then delivered the payoff: "There are no common law crimes."

And there it was. Brunelle couldn't help but frown. If they lost, it would be because of that fundamental principle of criminal law.

"No common law crimes," Milliken repeated. He pointed to the law books that filled the far wall of the courtroom. "Crimes are defined in those green books. The ones containing all of the statutes passed by our Legislature. Those other books, the tan ones containing over a century of appellate court decisions, contain discussion of those criminal statutes, application of those criminal statutes, even interpretation of those criminal statutes, but they do not, cannot, and should not contain the creation of those criminal statutes. The laws that send men to prison must be clear, precise, and crafted in the deliberative daylight of the legislative process. Citizens must have fair notice, in advance, of what actions can result in the loss of their liberty. And it is for this reason, that courts may never and must never craft new crimes in the common law that stems from their decisions."

"No common law crimes," Milliken repeated. He jutted a righteous finger into the air. "And no common law defenses."

"He's got a point," Carlisle whispered to Brunelle. He didn't know if it was to mess with him or to motivate him.

"Shh," Brunelle whispered back. He didn't need motivation and he certainly didn't need distraction.

Milliken lowered his hand. "Which brings me to the defense of duress. The State Legislature had codified, as they should have, the defense of duress at Revised Code of Washington 9A.16.060. Indeed, Chapter 9A.16 is titled 'Defenses,' and it is dedicated entirely to the enumeration and definition of legal defense to crimes. It is there, and should only be there, that the defense of duress is defined."

Milliken snatched a piece of paper from his table and held it up with a professorial flair. "So, let us examine the text of RCW 9A.16.060."

Judge Parmenter leaned forward and smiled slightly, as if to say, '*Oh, yes, let's.*'

"'In any prosecution for a crime,'" Milliken read aloud, "'it is a defense that the actor participated in the crime under compulsion by another, who by threat or use of force, created an apprehension in the mind of the actor that in case of refusal, he or she or another would be liable to immediate death or immediate grievous bodily injury.' Further, the statute states that 'such apprehension was reasonable' and 'the actor would not have participated in the crime except for the duress involved.'"

Milliken paused and nodded. "That is the defense. It makes sense, and our Legislature, good and wise, spelled it out clearly and concretely for all to understand and know."

He lifted the paper again and grinned. "But there is an exception. There is always an exception. What I read was subsection one of the statute. But there is a subsection two which limits the application of subsection one. Subsection two states, 'The defense of duress is not available if the crime charged is murder, manslaughter, or homicide by abuse.'"

Milliken set the paper back down on his table. "That limitation makes sense, Your Honor. It would also make sense not to have it. But our Legislature, in its wisdom, decided that the result of an illegal homicide would always, as a matter of law, be worse than whatever evil might result if the actor refused to act under duress. A person cannot, under this law, choose to take another person's life to save their own. Agree or disagree on the policy, that is what the law says. And," another dramatic pause, "that is all the law says."

Milliken took another moment, ostensibly to collect his thoughts and tug his suit coat back into place. Brunelle knew it was really to allow his last statement to sink in, and build the anticipation for what he would say next.

"That law, in its current form, was adopted in 1975," Milliken started up again. "And that law, in that form was applied as written for nearly thirty years, until an appellate court, faced with a case not dissimilar to the one that comes before Your Honor today, decided to ignore the prohibition against common law crimes, and by extension common law defenses, and added words to the statute which were not there, and importantly— very importantly—still are not there. In 2003, in the case of *State versus Mannering*, our State Supreme Court overstepped and purported to add the phrase, 'or attempted murder' to RCW 9A.16.060. And in all the intervening years, during annual session after annual session, our Legislature, in whom resides the power to define crimes and defenses, has never added that phrase to the statute. It was not what they intended in 1975. It was not what they intended in 2003. And it is not what they intend now."

Brunelle tapped his pen impatiently on his notepad. He had taken some notes when Milliken first started talking, but the more he listened to his opponent, the less he wanted to memorialize his arguments any further.

"Hard facts make bad law," Milliken continued. "It's a truth that we in the legal profession are all too aware of. A case with a difficult fact pattern makes its way up to an appellate court that doesn't like the result the law requires. So, instead of ruling under the law and letting the Legislature fix it, they try to fix it themselves. That never works out. And it hasn't worked out here.

The court in *Mannering* didn't want the defendant to get away with what he had done. Should he have been convicted?" A shrug. "I don't know. And it doesn't matter. What matters is that the *Mannering* court took away the jury's right to decide the defendant's guilt or innocence based on the criminal law as adopted by our elected representatives. That was wrong, and I urge this Honorable Court not to make the same mistake. Thank you."

Milliken sat down again to a smattering of applause from the defense attorneys in the gallery. People weren't supposed to clap, but defense attorneys made their living justifying breaking the rules.

"Enough of that." Parmenter frowned at the noise, gesturing for its cessation. "This isn't a political debate. This is a court of law. We deal in great and weighty matters here. I will have none of that." Once the courtroom was quiet again, he turned to the prosecutors. "I will hear now from the State."

And I will get no applause, Brunelle thought ruefully to himself as he stood. Although he knew he was also insulated from earning less applause than Milliken.

"Thank you, Your Honor," Brunelle began. "I will be brief, as brief as I can while still explaining why this Court should decline to overrule established precedent that has been applied to countless other defendants since the Supreme Court's clarification of RCW 9A.16.060 in its *Mannering* decision."

A lot of advocacy was about word choice. Milliken said the Supreme Court modified the duress statute. Brunelle said they clarified it. Parmenter's decision would come down to that distinction.

"There is a reason," Brunelle continued, "why the Supreme Court's decision in *Mannering* has endured all this time.

Indeed, it is the same reason the Legislature has not acted to add the phrase 'attempted murder' to the statute since that decision. And the reason is that it is not necessary. The Supreme Court's decision in *Mannering* did not do violence to the criminal statutes. It gave voice to them. All of them. For while counsel for the defendant wants this Court to analyze the duress statute in isolation, it does not exist in isolation. It is only one statute of dozens in Chapter 9A.16, and it is only one of hundreds in the criminal statutes adopted in Title 9 'Crimes and Punishments,' Title 9A 'Criminal Code,' and Title 10 'Criminal Procedure,' not to mention the crimes defined in the Title 46 'Traffic Code' and elsewhere in our state's criminal statutory system.

"The *Mannering* court, as should this Court, looked beyond the limited words in the duress statute itself and effectuated the Legislature's intent that attempted murder also be excluded from the duress defense. They explained that there is no separate crime of 'attempted murder.' Rather, another statute, RCW 9A.28.020 says that a person is guilty of attempting to commit a crime if, with the intent to commit that crime, they perform any act that is a substantial step toward the commission of that crime."

Brunelle didn't quote the statute verbatim from a cheat sheet. He didn't need to. Every criminal trial attorney knew the basic definition of an attempted crime. He might have gotten a word or two wrong, but he got the overall meaning correct.

"The definition of attempted murder is dependent on the definition of murder," Brunelle explained. "Therefore, any defense that is excluded for murder is also excluded for attempted murder. That is what the totality of the criminal statutes say, and that's what our Supreme Court said in *Mannering*. There is nothing nefarious or convoluted about that decision. It merely explained what the law always has been since duress was codified. It was the law then and it is the law now, and this Court should deny the defendant's motion to ignore settled precedent. Thank you."

No applause for Brunelle. He told himself it was because of Judge Parmenter's admonition. He knew it was also in part because he wasn't as theatrical nor as long-winded as Milliken. Carlisle at least gave him a pat on the shoulder.

"Solid effort," she said.

Not exactly the ringing endorsement Brunelle would have liked.

"Mr. Milliken, this is your motion, so you get the last word," Judge Parmenter said. "But I wonder if I might ask you a question or two, rather than simply be the audience for your advocacy."

Milliken stood to answer. "Of course, Your Honor. Whatever the Court wishes."

That was the right answer, of course, Brunelle knew.

"What say you to Mr. Brunelle's argument," the judge asked first, "that I should consider all of the criminal statutes as a whole, rather than focus solely on RCW 9A.16.060 as you seem to argue?"

"I agree wholeheartedly with Mr. Brunelle on that particular point," Milliken answered. "And when you do, please note that there are myriad other statutes that include or exclude attempted crimes specifically and explicitly, rather than rely on the sort of interpretive contortions championed by the State. The definition of a strike offense in RCW 9.94A.030. The definitions of violent offense or criminal street gang activity. Indeed, the punishment for attempted crimes are different from completed crimes, again by statute. How could it be that the definition of crimes and the punishments therefor are explicit in statute, but the defenses to them are not?"

Parmenter nodded without necessarily showing agreement. "And then, I know this is a purely legal motion, but I can't help but think that the particular facts of a case can help define the boundaries of the law that might apply to it. Have you provided the State with discovery of the facts you intend to rely on in the event I grant your motion?"

Milliken lifted his chin slightly. "I have not, Your Honor. I am only obligated to provide information I expect to use at trial. Until and unless the Court grants my motion, I cannot so expect. I can say, however, that I have prepared the information in anticipation of a favorable ruling. Furthermore, Mr. Brunelle is aware of the general facts as he was present when my client gave a preliminary explanation for his actions to law enforcement."

Parmenter looked to Brunelle for confirmation.

"That is correct, Your Honor," Brunelle stood to say. "I am aware generally of the facts underpinning the defendant's duress claim. Nothing in that changes the law."

The judge pursed his lips and nodded, then turned back to Milliken.

"It seems to me," he said, "that much of what both attorneys have argued is supported by both law and reason. There is, I believe, a reasonable chance that this issue may reach the appellate courts again if this case should go up on appeal."

Brunelle hoped so. An appeal meant a conviction. He couldn't appeal an acquittal.

"And I think," Parmenter continued, "that this is an important issue which should be decided on the fullest possible record."

Uh-oh. Brunelle, still standing, frowned down at Carlisle.

She frowned back.

"And that record will be less if I deny the motion," Parmenter continued, "because, as Mr. Milliken correctly explained, he is under no obligation to provide information that would be inadmissible at trial if I were to rule the duress defense unavailable to his client."

Brunelle steeled himself for the ruling.

"Therefore," Judge Parmenter declared, "I am going to do the following. First, I will keep this case for the trial. I think a continuity of judicial officers will be important to preserve the continuity of my rulings on this subject. Second, I will divide my ruling into a legal ruling and a factual ruling. Legally, I hereby grant the defendant's motion and rule that the duress defense is available, notwithstanding the State Supreme Court's rulings on the matter."

Shit, Brunelle made sure not to say it out loud.

"But," Parmenter continued, "I do not have enough information before me to decide whether the defendant's claims, if true, would meet the requirements of that defense. Mr. Milliken, you are to provide to the State any and all information regarding this defense within two weeks. Mr. Brunelle, you are free to provide any facts you think argue against the duress defense. Then we will see how things unfold at trial."

"Thank you very much, Your Honor," Milliken gloated, "for the Court's well-reasoned and just ruling."

"Understood, Your Honor." Brunelle could hardly thank the judge. He sat down again.

"Grunwald can say whatever he wants on the stand," Carlisle complained in his ear, "and Jacoby can't rebut it because he's in a coma. Milliken will make sure Grunwald provides enough facts to get the duress defense to the jury."

Brunelle nodded. "I know."

"So, what are we going to do?" Carlisle demanded.

"We need to get our own facts," Brunelle answered. "Better facts."

"From where?"

Brunelle turned to her and smiled. "Owl Road."

CHAPTER 21

In the event, they did not go to Owl Road, largely because there was no Owl Road. But there was a 37th Street, and on 37th Street there was a bar, and in that bar there was a regular who knew more than he'd been willing to share with Brunelle when they first met. Brunelle intended to remedy that. And he brought it back up.

"I'm sorry, what's the plan again?" Carlisle asked as they stood outside the door to The Purple Pig. "I mean, I know you explained it. I just don't know why you think it will work."

"Because it has to," Brunelle answered. "We're out of options and this is our best lead."

"Owl Road?" Carlisle questioned.

"Owl Road," Brunelle confirmed.

"Which we are now convinced is not an actual road?" Carlisle added.

"Exactly," Brunelle replied. "You understand perfectly."

Carlisle shook her head. "Fine. Whatever. You just better have my back."

"I do," Brunelle assured her. "Knock 'em dead."

Carlisle rolled her eyes, then pulled the door open and threw herself inside. Brunelle followed at a distance and slipped into a booth on the far side of the restaurant while Carlisle marched to the bar. Brunelle wished she would walk a little more ladylike, but he never would have said that to her. And it didn't matter anyway. The man from the previous night was there again with his eyes glued to his phone again. Carlisle hesitated and, Brunelle was pretty sure, shivered, then she took the seat next to him.

Brunelle couldn't hear what they were saying. They were too far away and the tavern was too loud. But he could see Carlisle initiate the conversation and the man hesitate, then lay his phone aside, albeit reluctantly, it appeared. Brunelle could also read their body language. Carlisle was forcing herself to be forward, aggressive even. The man was cautious. But he was still a man. And even though Carlisle wasn't interested in men, she had the looks that made men interested in her.

A waitress came to welcome Brunelle and ask if he was ready to order a drink. He was more than ready for that, but he wouldn't be staying long enough to enjoy it. He asked her for a bit more time, then returned his attention to Carlisle and her target. Brunelle's target anyway. She was more the arrow.

The man started to relax and opened his posture to Carlisle. He even smiled, which was something he hadn't even come close to when Brunelle had spoken with him ever so briefly on the previous occasion. Carlisle, for her part, seemed to be acting more naturally as well. Trial attorneys were performers, after all. She just needed a few minutes to find her character. Then it was time for Brunelle to enter, stage left.

Brunelle stormed across the tavern and grabbed the man

by the shoulder, pulling him violently to face him. The man's face was satisfyingly shocked.

"Just what do you think you're doing with my gal, buddy?" Brunelle demanded, ignoring that he had delivered the line like a 1940s gumshoe. Apparently, he needed more rehearsals.

"What?" the man squeaked. "Nothing. I mean," he looked at Carlisle, who raised an expectant eyebrow, "we were just talking."

"That's how it starts," Brunelle barked back.

"Come on, Mikey," Carlisle rested a hand on Brunelle's arm. "You said I could go out and play."

Mikey? Brunelle wondered at the name choice, but appreciated Carlisle's commitment to the part.

"You gotta pick better toys, Cassandra," he returned. He still had a hold of the techie's shoulder. "How am I supposed to respect you if you don't got no self-respect?"

"Can I say something?" the techie asked.

"No," Brunelle and Carlisle replied in unison.

But then Brunelle appended his answer. "Actually, yeah, you can say something. But you're gonna say it outside."

By this time, their theatrics had attracted the attention of those nearest them, not least of whom was Tim the Bartender. While tech workers might not be used to interacting with actual human beings at any depth worth remembering, the best bartenders made their living remembering their customers.

"Hey." Tim pointed to Brunelle. "You're the Manhattan guy from the other night."

That jarred the techie's memory. "Hey, yeah."

"Save it, Romeo!" Brunelle grabbed the man's shoulder harder and pulled him off his barstool. "Let's settle this outside."

The tech guy did not look in the slightest bit interested in settling anything outside. He didn't seem to be much of a lover, despite the setup, but he looked even less to be a fighter. Thin arms and pale skin shrunk under his dress shirt and outerwear vest combination. But he was still trying to figure out exactly what was going on. So, Carlisle knew how to scramble his thought again.

She reached out and laid a hand on the man's wrist. "This is all for my benefit, handsome. He knows it gets my motor running. Come outside and he'll let you take me for a test drive."

Brunelle hated that men could be so easily and predictably manipulated. But a career dealing with the worst thing people did to each other had led him to accept the things he might want to change. He was as guilty of it as any man, he knew. He had no qualms weaponizing it for the greater good.

"Uh…" the techie's jaw slowly fell open.

Brunelle released his grip even as Carlisle tightened hers. "Come with me," she insisted.

The man gave in and complied. He let Carlisle pull him toward the exit. He even forgot about his phone. Brunelle picked it up, then looked to Tim.

"He's not coming back in," Brunelle said. "Do you need me to settle his tab?"

Tim grinned. "The show was more than enough payment. Just promise you'll come again to tell me what the hell that was all about."

"Deal," Brunelle agreed, then he hurried after Carlisle and tech guy before the latter tried anything.

When Brunelle got outside, it was clear tech guy had immediately done exactly that. At the end of the building, just before the pedestrian alleyway that led to the tavern's garbage cans, Carlisle had him pinned against the brick wall, a forearm pressing into his throat. "Try that again, jerk," she growled. "There's no witnesses out here."

"Actually, there's one," Brunelle announced his arrival.

"Two." Chen stepped from the shadows of the alleyway.

"Whoa." The techie rasped and raised his arms. "This is getting too weird for me. I'm out. Find some other plaything."

"Toy," Brunelle corrected, "and yeah, that was all garbage. You never had a chance with her, for more reasons than one."

The tech guy frowned at Brunelle, then Carlisle, then Chen. "I wouldn't say I had no chance," he protested. Insisting on his virility to the last.

"I would." Carlisle pulled her arm back and shoved him against the wall.

"What the hell is going on?" the man demanded. Then he realized what was not in his pocket but was very visibly in Brunelle's hand. "Hey, give me my phone back!"

Brunelle looked at the device, but shook his head. "Hey, detective," he nodded at Chen. "Do we need a warrant to search abandoned property?"

"Detective?" the man called out. "Search? Oh no. No, you can't search my phone."

He made a move toward Brunelle, but Carlisle returned her forearm to his throat. "No sudden moves. This is an active crime scene."

"Crime scene?" he gasped. "What crime?"

"Aiding and abetting murder," Brunelle answered. "Well, attempted murder, anyway. That's still, what? Forty years in prison?" he asked Carlisle dramatically.

"Thirty-five," Carlisle answered. "Unless the victim dies

tonight. Then it's life."

The actual sentences for the crimes contemplated weren't any of those; they were considerably less. But Tech Guy didn't know that.

"How's the victim doing anyway?" Brunelle asked.

Chen shook his head solemnly. "Not good. Not good at all." He looked at their subject. "You're not going to like prison."

The man threw his hands up. "What in the hell is going on? I just came here for my usual drink on my way home."

"Home from where?" Brunelle demanded.

"My job," the man answered.

"Where do you work?" Brunelle followed up.

"MegaThink," he answered. "The tech company. I work at their new campus down by the water."

Brunelle decided to take a risk. The man would never be as receptive as he was right then. "Does The Owl work there too?"

Anticipation crackled between Brunelle, Carlisle, and Chen as they waited to see if Brunelle's gambit would pay off.

"The Owl?" The man laughed. "You don't know anything about The Owl."

Brunelle knew then that there was an Owl. That was already a win. But he wasn't one to be satisfied with a single victory.

"But you do," Brunelle said, "and you're going to tell us everything you know."

"Why would I do that?" the man replied. "I don't even know who you are."

Brunelle thought for a moment. He looked at Carlisle. She shrugged. Then he looked to Chen. He nodded.

"Fine," Brunelle said. "First, you tell us your name. Then,

we tell you why we need the information. And if all goes well, you get your phone back and go home." When the man hesitated, Brunelle nodded back toward the pub entrance and added, "I've already settled up your bill."

The man seemed to appreciate that, probably more than he should have under all of the circumstances. "Okay," he agreed.

Carlisle let him go again and stood back onto the curb.

"My name is Aiden Barnaby. Happy now?" He nodded toward Carlisle. "I would have told her that without being assaulted."

"That was just recreational," Carlisle responded. "I don't care what your name is."

"Who is The Owl?" Brunelle returned everyone to task. "And what does 1900 Owl Road mean?"

"I don't know his real name," Barnaby insisted. "And I don't know why you keep asking about an Owl Road. There is no Owl Road, just The Owl."

Carlisle frowned and stepped forward. "Owl R.D. Not Owl Road. Owl R.D. What does that mean?"

Barnaby thought for a moment, then his face lit up in recognition. "I don't know," he obviously lied.

Carlisle took an angry step at him, and he recoiled into the brick behind him.

"It's not an address," Brunelle finally pulled it all together. "Nineteen-hundred is a time, not a house number. Meet The Owl at seven p.m. But for what? What is R.D.?"

Barnaby didn't reply. That confirmed he knew exactly what it stood for.

Brunelle held up Barnaby's phone. "This is your last chance to help us. What are we going to find on this phone if you don't?"

That seemed to give Barnaby pause. But then he shook his head. "He'll kill me."

"For real?" Carlisle asked.

"Well, no," Barnaby admitted. "But I mean, maybe. I don't know. He's into some pretty dark stuff. I don't really know what he's capable of."

"Well, you know what we're capable of," Brunelle said. "Me and the lady are with the D.A.'s office. The man with the gun and handcuffs is a cop. We're working on an attempted murder case where the victim met with The Owl about something abbreviated 'R.D.' You obviously know what that stands for, so if you refuse to help us, you could be charged with a whole host of crimes, from obstructing to accomplice to murder. So, please, just tell us what R.D. stands for and why a plastic surgeon in the ICU would be meeting with someone who doesn't even use his real name."

Barnaby thought for several seconds. "I know what R.D. stands for."

"What?" Carlisle demanded. She jabbed a thumb at Brunelle. "He's the good cop. You know what that makes me. And I am all out of patience."

Barnaby actually managed a slight smile. "Maybe after this, I can buy you that drink after all?"

Carlisle went for his throat again, literally, but Brunelle stepped between them. "Don't push your luck, Barnaby. Just tell us what R.D. stands for and we're done with you."

Barnaby smiled a bit more fully at Carlisle, then dropped the smile again and looked to Brunelle. "Real Delete. That's what it stands for. It's a program that deletes files from your computer so that they're really gone, not just waiting to be overwritten. It's not the kind of stuff normal people need. It's definitely the sort of thing criminals use. That's why he goes by a fake name. But he's also kind of a legend, so if you work in this area, you've probably heard of him."

Brunelle believed Barnaby. He looked to his partners. "Are we done with him?"

Carlisle and Chen both agreed that they were, and Brunelle handed him his phone back. "You better have told us the truth. We have your name now. We can track you down."

Barnaby snatched his phone from Brunelle's hand. Then he leaned toward Carlisle. "I don't think I got your name."

"Go fuck yourself," Carlisle replied.

"That's with one K," Brunelle added. "Get out of here."

Barnaby decided not to press his luck any further and scurried away, passing the entrance to The Purple Pig and disappearing around the corner.

"Real Delete," Chen repeated the name of the computer program Barnaby had described. "That checks out with what Houser told us. Grunwald was using a program like that to delete the files off his computer."

"The emails from the supposed blackmailers," Carlisle added.

"Yeah." Brunelle nodded. "So, why was Jacoby meeting with him?"

CHAPTER 22

They couldn't ask Jacoby why he was meeting with an underground computer programmer. He was still in a coma at Harborview. So, they needed to talk to the other party to the meeting. The computer programmer. The Owl.

"The Owl?" Houser practically squealed when Brunelle, Carlisle, and Chen briefed him on what they had learned from Aiden Barnaby. "He's real? That's awesome."

"Maybe not that awesome," Brunelle cautioned. "He's wrapped up in some dark stuff, not least of which is attempted murder."

"Right, right," Houser agreed less than convincingly. "It's just, I've heard of this guy. I just didn't think he was real. But it actually explains a lot of what I've seen on a couple of cases recently. See, there was this one where—"

"Can we stay focused on my case?" Brunelle asked. Then, with a nod to Carlisle, "Or case. This case. The Grunwald case. We need to talk to The Owl."

"We need to do more than that," Carlisle put in. "If he

provided the means for Grunwald to delete those emails he claimed he got, then that makes him an accomplice."

"I should probably remind everyone," Brunelle put in, "that our working theory is that Grunwald is lying about that. And I think the fact that Jacoby was the one meeting The Owl, and not Grunwald, supports our theory. But we need this Owl guy to confirm it."

"He's not going to just meet with a bunch of prosecutors and cops," Houser pointed out.

Brunelle grinned. "That's where you come in."

Houser tipped his head at Brunelle. "What can I do?"

"You can contact this Owl," Brunelle answered, "and set up a meeting."

Houser frowned at the suggestion, but he didn't say no.

"Do you know how to contact him?" Brunelle asked.

Houser thought for a bit. "Well, now that I know he's real, maybe."

"Maybe?" Chen questioned.

"Probably," Houser amended. "What did your informant say the program was called again?"

"I'm not sure he was an informant," Brunelle hedged, "but he said it was called 'Real Delete.'"

Houser nodded. "Okay. The Owl is real and I know the name of his deletion program." He hurried over to one of the several open laptops on his workstation. "It's going to take me some time, but I can probably track him down. I'll need to set up a fake identity with a ghost ISP and—"

"We don't need to know the details," Brunelle interrupted. "We just need to know the where and when."

"Okay," Houser agreed. "How much time do I have?"

"Not much," Carlisle answered. "Trial is in less than a

month."

"Can you win the trial without The Owl?" Houser asked.

"Not unless Jacoby dies," Brunelle answered.

"Whoa, bad karma," Chen responded. He nodded to Houser's workbench. "Knock on wood or something."

Brunelle looked at the wood he should knock on to keep Jacoby alive. "I think I won't. I need every advantage now."

CHAPTER 23

Houser said it would probably take about two weeks to set up a meeting with The Owl. He explained the reasons why it took so long to Brunelle. Something about chat rooms, intermediaries, bona fides, and of course, money. Brunelle didn't care much about the details, except that they be written down somewhere to provide to Milliken as discovery once Brunelle had successfully sprung his trap and gathered the additional facts he needed to defeat Grunwald's bogus duress defense at trial.

While they waited, Brunelle had other work to do, but he did his best to do it anywhere but in his office. He was avoiding Lang. He didn't want to find himself in a compromising position that could have negative impacts on his office. But he was also avoiding someone far more important to his long-term career.

"Dave. There you are." Matt Duncan's voice slipped over Brunelle's shoulder as he sat huddled in the corner of the courthouse law library. "Fancy meeting you here," he added with a laugh.

There wasn't much humor in the laugh, but it wasn't

totally bereft of warmth. Brunelle supposed he should be grateful for that. He looked up from his file and turned around to face his boss.

"Matt." He made sure to smile broadly. *Probably too broadly,* he thought after he did it. He patted the papers in front of him. "I just wanted someplace quiet to really sink my teeth into this Grunwald case, you know?"

"If you want someplace quiet," Duncan replied, "I can recommend your office. It seems like no one's been in there at all since you went behind my back and added Gwen to your case."

Brunelle fought to hold his grin. "Right. Well, um, I came to talk to you again, but you were busy, and then the hearing was coming up. I did talk to Ms. Lang, sort of. But anyway, the case is getting a little twisty now. We lost a preliminary hearing about the duress defense and—"

"Yeah, I heard about that." Duncan frowned.

Brunelle was fairly certain he wasn't about to get fired. He'd worked there too long and accomplished too much to get summarily dismissed for one bad decision. A lot of what he'd accomplished over that long time came from making a bad decision here and there. But there were a lot of things Duncan could do to make Brunelle's professional life unpleasant if he wanted to, beginning with pulling the Grunwald case from him. Not only had Brunelle added Carlisle without permission, he'd lost the most important battle short of the actual trial and made the trial that much harder in the process.

"That was a bullshit ruling," Duncan finally added. "Parmenter is too smart for his own good sometimes."

Brunelle exhaled. "We're not licked yet," he insisted.

Duncan nodded. "I've known you long enough to know that. I've also known you long enough to know you were going to bring Gwen onto the case whether I agreed or not. Honestly, it took you longer than I thought it would."

"Oh." Brunelle smiled. "Thanks for understanding."

"I also know you well enough to know there's something off about the way you and that woman from the auditor's office interact," Duncan added. "Please don't mess that up, Dave. A bad report from her will affect a lot more people than just you and me. Keep her happy. Whatever it takes, keep her happy."

Brunelle wasn't so sure about whatever it took to keep Lang happy, but he was willing to offer at least some assurance.

"Don't worry, Matt," he replied. "I'll make sure she understands how important our work is."

"Glad to hear it." Duncan nodded. "So, is Gwen the secret ingredient that's going to make sure you win the case?"

Brunelle shrugged. "She's important, I can say that much. But I'm still working on the secret ingredient."

Duncan smiled. "You have something up your sleeve?"

"Always," Brunelle replied. "Although this trick is more memory cards than playing cards."

Duncan narrowed his eyes. "I'm not sure what that's supposed to mean, but it sounds like you know. Win the case, Dave, and send Marietta away happy. Can you do those two things for me?"

"I can win the case, Matt," Brunelle answered.

As for Marietta Lang, he thought, *she's going to have to learn to take no for an answer.*

CHAPTER 24

Houser's answer came exactly two weeks before trial was set to begin. The computer expert summoned Brunelle to his workplace. Carlisle couldn't make it; she was in court. Chen couldn't make it; he was out on a call. And Brunelle couldn't wait for them; he was more than ready to take on The Owl.

"So, it took a little more work than I expected," Houser explained. "I found some good chat groups, but it took forever to get directed to the one where this Owl guy was. I had to ask permission to join, and even after I got that, I had to wait for him to post. But then—"

"I don't care," Brunelle interrupted. "Did you schedule a time to meet?"

"Well, yes, but—" Houser tried to protest.

"Just tell me the when and where," Brunelle said. "I can get the how later, if it matters."

"I think it matters," Houser muttered, at least half to himself.

"When and where?" Brunelle insisted.

"Tomorrow night," Houser answered, failing at whatever attempt he was making to conceal his disappointment. "Twenty-one-hundred hours. Under the Fremont Bridge."

"Walking distance from MegaThink's Fremont campus," Brunelle noted aloud. "Thanks, Jack."

The Owl was probably some tech guy already making more in a year than Brunelle would in ten as a government employee. And the jerk still had a side hustle selling illicit computer programs to would-be murderers.

Or, for reasons Brunelle hadn't figured out yet, to their victims.

The plan was similar to the night they confronted Aiden Barnaby, except Houser would be the bait instead of Carlisle, and Chen would be the one swooping in, not Brunelle. It was a police operation, not lawyers playing cops and robbers. That didn't mean Brunelle wouldn't be nearby. Houser was wired up and Brunelle was listening in two blocks away at a different bar whose name wasn't important except that it not be The Purple Pig. Barnaby was a regular there and he didn't want to be spotted; that could ruin everything if he put two and two together and had a way to warn off The Owl. Carlisle had also opted to stay home and receive updates via text. But all of that didn't mean Brunelle was alone, despite his best efforts.

"Dave?"

Brunelle recognized the voice. He had taken up a table near the window and was looking intently into the dark, as if he would be able to see through the forest of buildings between where he was sitting and where Houser would rendezvous with The Owl. He hadn't been paying attention to the remainder of his surroundings. He should have.

He turned and faced the woman standing over him, drink

in hand and grin on face. He nodded up at her. "Ms. Lang."

"Oh, my God. Call me Marietta." She sat down at his table without asking. "Small world. What are you doing here?"

There was no way Brunelle was going to explain what he was really doing there. "Uh, you know, just getting a drink after work."

Lang looked at the time. "Did you really work until almost nine o'clock at night?" She leaned over and put a hand on his arm. "You are so dedicated."

He was still working, of course. But he didn't tell her that, of course.

"Yes, well, justice and all that," he replied, slipping his arm out from under her hand. "It was nice to run into you. I'm sure you have other places to be."

"We're in the same place, silly." She laughed. She had a very nice laugh.

"Other people to be with, then," he tried.

Lang smiled. She had a very nice smile. "I'd much rather be with you, Dave."

Brunelle sighed to himself. She was right that it was almost nine o'clock. He had an earpiece in one ear. He had been monitoring the final conversations between Houser and Chen, but they had gone quiet in anticipation of the meeting, and the ambient noise of the bar made it difficult to hear anything without focusing. Lang made it impossible to focus.

"So, do you live around here?" She glanced vaguely toward the neighborhood on the other side of the windows. "I'm just kind of exploring the city. Someone said Fremont had the best craft beers."

She raised her glass of orangey-yellow suds. Brunelle deduced it wasn't her first, based on the fuzziness at the edges of her speech and movements. She wasn't drunk, but she wasn't sober either.

Brunelle had a decision to make. Duncan had told him to keep Lang happy. But Brunelle also wanted her to go away. Reminding her that he lived with his girlfriend, in the suburbs or not, would probably serve the latter goal but potentially undermine the former. He could simply say, 'No,' and leave Casey out of it, allowing the conversation to continue for however long and winding that might be. Or he could specifically remind Lang of Casey and hope she left in a huff.

He settled on his decision, but then events rescued him from its execution. Houser's voice crackled in his ear, thin and barely audible, but there. And important. More important in that moment than whatever Lang wanted from him.

Brunelle pressed the earpiece into his ear and stood up. "I'm sorry. I have to go."

Lang's expression dropped. She forced a laugh. "Was it something I said?"

"No, no," he assured her. He pointed to the earpiece. "Work stuff. I guess my day isn't over yet after all."

He hadn't even had a chance to order a drink before being accosted by Lang, so there was no bill to settle up. He hurried toward the exit, finger pressed against the earpiece.

"...thanks for meeting me," Houser was saying. "I thought maybe we would do this over email or something."

"I know better than to link our two computers," The Owl replied, his voice distant and tinny in Houser's microphone. "Whatever you need this for, I don't want to be traced to it."

"It's, it's nothing illegal," Houser claimed in a tone that made it seem like it was something very illegal. "I brought the money."

"Good," The Owl replied. "Set it down over—"

The rest of The Owl's instructions were drowned out by the demand shrieked from inches behind him.

"Just who the hell do you think you are, David Brunelle?"

Brunelle turned around to find Marietta Lang scowling at him. That second beer was no longer in her hand, but was almost certainly making its way into her blood stream. He didn't really have time for this, but he couldn't stop himself from making a quip that would not help bring matters to a quick resolution.

"That kind of answers itself, doesn't it?"

Lang frowned. Even buzzed and angry, she had a very nice frown. "I don't know what that means. I just know that I have been very nice to you, and you haven't been nice to me at all."

The anger fell from her expression like snow off a branch. Left behind was sadness. "And I don't know why."

Brunelle was pretty sure she knew exactly why. Or at least that she should be able to figure it out. He might not have a ring on his finger but he was a taken man. He felt like he probably comported himself as such. Either he was wrong about that or she didn't care. More importantly, he had other more pressing matters at hand.

"I can't really do this right now," he told her, even as he tried to listen to what was happening between Houser and The Owl.

"...thumb drive...it will do what you want it to...refunds...don't try to find me again..."

"Why not?" Lang complained. "You keep avoiding me. That's not very nice. And it's not very smart. Matt wouldn't like it."

"Matt?" Brunelle's attention was sufficiently divided that he didn't recognize the name out of context. He'd never gone drinking or on a stake out with his boss.

"Mr. Duncan," Lang clarified. "He assigned you to me for a reason. I can't help it if I like my assignment."

Brunelle knew there was a compliment in there somewhere, and also that it was probably inappropriate. He also knew Houser was laying the groundwork for the arrest of The Owl.

"…this is really going to help me…can't let the cops find that stuff…I'd never be able to do it without you…"

The Owl, for his part, voice distant but intelligent, tried to avoid any responsibility for what was to be done with his creation.

"…not interested in what you're going to use it for…it's just a tool…I'm just a businessman…"

"Uh, okay," Brunelle said, turning slightly away and pressing the earpiece deeper into his ear. "Look, can we talk about this later, maybe? I'm a little distracted right now."

Lang didn't reply immediately. She just stared at Brunelle, and long enough that he noticed and looked back at her. She smiled. "Yes. Yes, we can definitely talk later. Promise?"

"Uh, yes. Sure. Whatever," Brunelle answered.

Lang did a little hop. "I know where we'll go. I found this great place near the waterfront. I'll book a table for next weekend. I can't wait."

Brunelle returned his focus to Lang quickly enough to watch her bound back into the restaurant, but not fast enough to protest what she had said before doing so. And any thought of going after her to clarify his intentions was eradicated by the sudden explosion of activity in his ear.

"…under arrest…stop!…he's getting away!…"

"Damn it," Brunelle hissed to himself. He turned and

started jogging toward the rendezvous point several blocks away.

"...got past Larry...coming your way, Dave...stop him..."

Brunelle increased his jog to a full-blown run, turning down 37th Street toward the water. He didn't see The Owl coming his way, but he did see a familiar face approaching on the sidewalk. Aiden Barnaby.

He must go to The Purple Pig every single night, Brunelle thought.

"Stop! Police!" Houser's voice could be heard rising up the hill behind Barnaby.

"That's him, Dave!" followed Chen's voice. "Barnaby! Barnaby's The Owl!"

Brunelle looked at Barnaby, who was only a few feet away from him. Barnaby looked at Brunelle, then jumped over the hedge to his right and sprinted toward the underground parking garage of a condominium complex. Brunelle dropped into a full sprint himself, hurdling the hedge far more effectively than he feared he might. Brunelle was no athlete, but neither was Barnaby, and Barnaby was already tired from his initial escape from Houser. Brunelle gained on him quickly, spurred on by the fear they might lose him in the garage.

As they reached the top of the driveway that led down into the parking garage, Brunelle could taste victory. A metal gate blocked the entry. Barnaby pulled up short. Brunelle slammed into him and propelled them both into the gate, with a loud enough crash that the actual cops would have no trouble finding them.

They tumbled to the ground. Brunelle knew he wasn't a commissioned law enforcement officer and didn't have the legal authority to arrest someone. The detectives' shouts to stop

Barnaby were unlikely to qualify as a field deputation, although he would have been willing to argue that, if need be. He guessed it would probably be more credible and equally effective to simply be a large man lying on top of a smaller man, remaining clumsily entangled long enough for the real cops to arrive with their handcuffs.

"Get off of me!" Barnaby huffed as he tried to squirm out from under Brunelle.

"Sorry," Brunelle replied. "Can't move. Heart condition."

Barnaby continued to struggle but to little avail. In moments, Houser and Chen arrived and had no trouble handcuffing Barnaby once Brunelle decided to find the energy to roll off of him.

Brunelle stood up and took a moment. His heart was racing still from just that short sprint, but he'd learned how to let it pass. He brushed himself off, then leaned down and looked at Barnaby, lying on his stomach, hands behind his back, and face raised to Brunelle's defiantly.

"You're The Owl?" Brunelle questioned, as if he couldn't believe it himself.

Barnaby sneered up at him. "Hoot."

Brunelle had to laugh. "That is not even close to intimidating," he informed him, "but it is absolutely a confession."

CHAPTER 25

Brunelle wanted more of a confession than just, 'Hoot.' That meant Barnaby was transported to the North Precinct, rather than directly to the King County Jail for booking. The North Precinct was smaller than the main precinct downtown, but it was closer, and it had an interrogation room. Rather than a two-way mirror, though, Brunelle had to watch via closed-circuit television. It was adequate, but lacked the intimacy of being on the other side of a thin sheet of glass from a murderer. Then again, Barnaby wasn't a murderer. He was just an amoral opportunist.

The room was a typical police interrogation room. A single small table with two chairs, all bolted to the floor lest a subject try to use them as a weapon. Barnaby sat in the corner, his right arm handcuffed to a metal loop bolted to the wall. It prevented him from being able to fully lower that arm into his lap, something that would become tiring after a while. A small technique to wear down suspects.

Another such technique was leaving the suspect alone in the room for an uncomfortable amount of time. It allowed their anxiety to rise with no outlet, wondering what the cops were doing and imagining worst case scenarios. By the time the interrogator entered the room, the suspect would be dying to talk to someone, anyone, and would try to talk their way out of those worst case scenarios. At least that was the plan.

When Chen finally entered the room to confront Barnaby, it didn't go according to plan.

"Nice to see you again, Mr. Barnaby," Chen began formally. Formality communicated the seriousness of the situation, while offering the nicety of pretending there was some equality of the power dynamic, despite one of them being shackled to a wall.

The truth was, Brunelle knew, Chen was in charge.

"I want a lawyer," Barnaby replied.

Or not, Brunelle appended his thought.

The one thing, the only thing, that could prevent a lengthy interrogation was the suspect invoking their right to an attorney. Chen could plow ahead, of course. He could ignore the request and question him anyway. He could obtain the most detailed confession in the history of law enforcement, but Brunelle would never be allowed to use it.

Chen knew that too, of course. He hadn't even sat down yet and the interrogation was over.

"Are you sure about that?" he asked. Even that question was problematic. A detective couldn't talk you out of your request for an attorney. They could, of course, but whatever you said after that would also be suppressed, tainted by the cop's effort to overcome your desire to assert your constitutional right to an attorney. The most Chen could do was clarify Barnaby's intent, which that question technically did, even if Chen's tone strongly suggested Barnaby should change his mind and talk to him.

"I am certain about that," Barnaby replied. "I will not talk to you without a lawyer."

He wouldn't talk to Chen with a lawyer, either, Brunelle knew. No criminal defense attorney would let their client talk to the cops. Not up-front, anyway. Not without some agreement in place. But that was fine with Brunelle.

He watched Chen nod at Barnaby, then leave the interrogation room. A few moments later, Chen walked into the observation room where Brunelle was.

"Well, that was fast," Chen said. "He invoked. I'm done. Anything you want me to do before I book him into jail?"

Brunelle grinned. "Yeah. Get him a lawyer."

Chen raised an eyebrow. "Now?"

"Sure," Brunelle answered. "Why not?"

"Because that's a complete waste of time," Chen answered. "We call the on-call public defender. They talk for way too long on the phone. Then Barnaby says he's not going to talk to me, which I already knew. And then I drive him to jail. We never do that. Suspect invokes, interrogation ends, straight to jail. You know that."

"I do know that." Brunelle nodded. "But Barnaby isn't the one I want to talk to anyway. I want to talk to his lawyer. So, let's go ahead and get him one."

Chen looked at his watch. "You're not going to be able to cut any deals with whatever random junior public defender is covering the phones tonight."

"True enough," Brunelle allowed. "So, we don't call a random junior public defender. We call a specific senior public defender."

* * *

"I can't believe you talked me into coming all the way out here," Jessica Edwards complained when she arrived at the North Precinct. She was wearing a hooded sweatshirt and jeans. "You're lucky I didn't have any plans tonight."

"We're old, Jess," Brunelle responded. "We don't have plans anymore. Not fun ones, anyway."

"So, what's going on here?" Edwards got right to business. "I might not have had plans, but I don't want to be up all night. What's such a big deal that you couldn't tell me the details over the phone? Or you couldn't just book the guy and let me be assigned at the arraignment tomorrow?"

"That's just it. I don't want to charge him," Brunelle answered. "Not with anything serious, anyway. I want him to be a witness, not a defendant. It's better for everyone if he does that willingly."

"What did he do?" Edwards asked. "Get rid of a murder weapon or something? Do you already have the murderer in custody or do you need this guy to identify him?"

"The attempted murderer is out on bail," Brunelle answered. "This guy sold him his defense. I want to blow that up."

Edwards took a moment, then her face lit up in recognition. "The plastic surgeon case? The one Milliken is on?"

"Yep, that one," Brunelle confirmed. "The shooter used a black market computer program to delete everything on his computer that would support, or undercut, his duress defense. The guy in the holding cell is the programmer who made it for him."

Edwards nodded. "Did he know what it was for when he sold it to him?"

Brunelle frowned slightly. "Well, that's a bit of a wrinkle.

We think he might have sold it to the victim, not the shooter. We tracked him down from a note in the victim's wallet."

Edwards raised an eyebrow. "That is a wrinkle. Computer guy sells illicit computer program to victim, but it ends up on the shooter's computer and erases everything that could be used to prove or disprove his defense."

"That's it exactly," Brunelle confirmed.

Edwards laughed. "No wonder you called me."

"Yes," Brunelle was about to compliment her lawyering skills.

"You totally need this guy or your case against Milliken is garbage," Edwards continued. "Oh yeah, you're going to give me everything I want. No charges, letter of apology, a week at a time share in Hawaii."

Brunelle put away that compliment he had ready. "Let's start with no charges." He crossed his arms. "But I need to know what he's going to testify to."

"Oh, so you want him to actually testify?" Edwards replied. "Not just snitch him out on tape. Yeah, let's make that two weeks in Hawaii."

"Let's make that two years in prison, if he doesn't help," Brunelle shot back.

But Edwards wasn't fazed. She'd been doing the defense thing as long as Brunelle had been doing the prosecution thing. "What do you even have on him? It's not a credible threat if you can't actually prove a crime. What are you going for? Rendering criminal assistance? Some sort of cybercrime?"

"I'll go accomplice to attempted murder, if I have to, Jess," Brunelle answered. "If he knew Grunwald was going to use his program to cover up a murder, then he goes down on the same charge."

"That's a pretty big if," Edwards returned, more seriously. "Especially when he sold his program to the victim, not the defendant."

"I know, I know." Brunelle climbed down a bit. "That's why I need to know what really happened. That's why you're here."

Chen walked up at that point. "Did you brief her on the situation, Dave?"

"He did," Edwards answered. "I'll go talk to him, but there's no way he gives a statement tonight. And no way he cooperates if you charge him with accomplice to attempted murder tomorrow."

"He ran from us when we tried to arrest him," Chen pointed out. "That's obstructing a law enforcement officer."

"Perfect," Brunelle said. "Obstructing is a misdemeanor. One charge of that to keep him honest, then after he agrees to testify and actually does so, we dismiss the charge."

Edwards shrugged. "We'll see. I need to talk to him first."

"But no way he makes a statement tonight, right?" Brunelle asked.

"Right," Edwards confirmed.

"Good," Brunelle answered. "I'm exhausted, and I still have to drive across the damn bridge. I'll see you tomorrow, Jess, at Barnaby's arraignment."

CHAPTER 26

Brunelle and Carlisle arrived in the courtroom a few minutes before the daily arraignment calendar was scheduled to begin. There were no cameras in the courtroom. No gallery full of curious onlookers of anxious families. Just prosecutors and defense attorneys, guards and defendants, and the judge, making the daily sausage. And no sign of Milliken.

"I still can't believe that jackass from the bar is really this Owl guy we were looking for," Carlisle remarked as they set their files on the prosecution table in front of the judge's bench. "We should charge him with false statement to a public servant for lying to us."

"It's not too late for that," Brunelle responded, "but let's hope it doesn't come to that. We just want a charge to hang over his head and have his right to court-appointed counsel attach. Then Jess walks him to our conference room for Chen to take a lengthy and thorough statement that confirms the computer deletion program was for anything other than deleting fake emails from fake dark-web blackmailers."

"You're putting a lot of faith in someone we know is a liar," Carlisle pointed out. "Milliken isn't going to go as easy on him as we did."

"Milliken isn't going to press an arm across his throat," Brunelle replied. "I'm sure he'll do fine."

Edwards walked into the courtroom at the exact same time as the judge. No time for greetings. Just a wave as the bailiff called out, "All rise! The King County Superior Court is now in session, The Honorable Janice Atchison presiding."

Brunelle winced at the name. He was hoping some other judge had rotated in since Grunwald's arraignment, but no such luck. Fortunately, it wasn't a serious charge and both sides were in agreement to release Barnaby on his personal recognizance. It would be a lot harder to conduct a clandestine proffer interview from a jail cell.

"Be seated," Atchison directed. "Do we have any matters rea—" she began. Then she spotted Brunelle, with Carlisle, and Edwards behind them. "Do we have a homicide case on the docket today? I don't recall seeing anything as serious as that."

Brunelle stepped forward. "No homicides today, Your Honor," he assured the judge. "We're here on the Aiden Barnaby matter."

Judge Atchison frowned as she looked down to consult her docket. "Obstructing?" she questioned after a moment. "That's a misdemeanor."

"Yes, Your Honor," Brunelle confirmed.

"This should be filed in the district court," Atchison complained, "not superior court."

Stand-alone misdemeanors were generally supposed to be filed in the lower district court. Superior court was for felonies and any misdemeanors that might have been committed at the same time. So, the judge had a point. But she didn't have all of the information.

"The State has its reasons for filing this charge in superior court, Your Honor," Brunelle responded. "And the superior court has jurisdiction over both felonies and misdemeanors. There is no legal prohibition against filing misdemeanors in superior court. In fact, a few of our least populous counties don't even have district courts; everything is filed in superior court."

"We are not one of the least populous counties, Mr. Brunelle," Judge Atchison scolded. "We are the most populous county. We have over fifty superior court judges whose paramount mission is the adjudication of felony criminal charges. Tell me why this case is taking up valuable time and space on my calendar."

They could have been done with the arraignment in the amount of time Atchison was complaining about the time it was taking up. But Brunelle knew not to say that.

"The defendant is agreeing to charges being filed in superior court, Your Honor," Edwards spoke up. "For reasons I am not at liberty to divulge at this time."

That gave the judge pause. She could, and would, demand answers from prosecutors all day, but defense attorneys were allowed to have secrets. And judges were supposed to respect those confidences.

"I see," Atchison said after a few seconds of reflection. She pulled herself up and stared down her nose at the lawyers beneath her. "Then we can address the Barnaby matter. The sooner the better, I dare say."

Brunelle nodded to the guard, who opened the secure door to the holding cells and called out, "Barnaby!" A few moments later, Barnaby entered the courtroom, dressed out in gray jail scrubs and looking the worse for wear after a night in the county jail. He seemed relieved to see Edwards again and joined her on the defense side of the bar.

"This is the matter of *The State of Washington versus Aiden Barnaby*," Brunelle formally called the case for the record. "David Brunelle and Gwen Carlisle, appearing on behalf of the State."

"Jessica Edwards, appearing on behalf of the accused, Aiden Barnaby," Edwards put in next. "The defense is ready to proceed with arraignment."

Judge Atchison still appeared visibly perturbed at being forced to deal with something as trivial as a misdemeanor, and a nonviolent one at that. "Yes, yes. Please proceed."

"The State is filing one charge of obstructing a law enforcement officer against the defendant," Brunelle declared as he handed the original of the criminal complaint to the bailiff. He handed two copies of it to Edwards. "We would ask the defense to acknowledge receipt of the complaint, waive formal reading of the charges, and enter a plea."

Edwards accepted the papers from Brunelle. "The defense acknowledges receipt of the complaint, waives a formal reading, and enters a plea of not guilty."

It was all very formal and rote.

"A plea of not guilty is entered," Atchison confirmed. "Mr. Brunelle, if there is any reason I should not release the defendant on his own recognizance, and I cannot imagine any such reason, please speak now. Otherwise, I will P.R. the defendant and we can be done with this hearing."

Brunelle shook his head. "The State has no objection to a personal recognizance release, Your Honor."

"The defendant is released on his own recognizance," the judge announced before Brunelle had even finished his sentence.

"Next case!"

"That was easy," Carlisle remarked in a low voice as they stepped away from the bar.

Brunelle knew it would be the easiest part of coercing Barnaby into helping them. As if to confirm as much, Edwards stepped over to them after shaking her client's hand and instructing him to call her upon being processed out and released.

"He's still not thrilled about doing this," she cautioned the prosecutors, "but if I think it's in his best interests, I'll get him to do it."

Brunelle frowned. "If?"

"I haven't seen the police reports, Dave," Edwards replied. "I'd love to take your word for it, and personally I do trust your word, but professionally I can't do that. I need to see what you've got against my client, and I'm also going to need to see what you've got against Grunwald. Then, if it all says what I think it will all say, I'll reach out and we'll schedule a time for my client to talk with you. After he signs his immunity agreement, of course."

Brunelle couldn't stifle a sigh.

"Are you sure it was a good idea to bring her on board?" Carlisle teased. "I bet a lawyer like Nick Lannigan wouldn't bother reading the police reports."

"Aiden Barnaby wouldn't listen to a lawyer like Nick Lannigan," Brunelle returned. Then, to Edwards, "I'll have my legal assistant rush those reports over to you, Jess. I want this proffer done as soon as possible. If Barnaby gives us what I want, we'll have to turn the transcript over to Milliken. I don't want to give him an excuse to delay the trial."

Edwards agreed to the plan and promised to contact them as soon as she had received and reviewed the reports. It was time for Brunelle and Carlisle to head back to their respective offices. As they left the courtroom, Brunelle did one last scan to confirm Milliken hadn't gotten wind of their plans and snuck in while they were on the record. Fortunately, Milliken wasn't there.

Less fortunately, Marietta Lang was.

Seated in the last row of the gallery, hidden among the friends and family of the defendants to be arraigned next, she stood as Brunelle and Carlisle approached the exit.

"We should talk," Lang said to Brunelle. "Alone."

Carlisle grinned at Brunelle. "Sounds good to me."

"What happened to being a witness?" Brunelle complained.

"I'm already on the case," she pointed out. "Just don't do anything you would need a witness for." He nodded to Lang. "Always nice to see you, Ms. Lang. Please don't fire any of us."

Carlisle slipped out of the courtroom and Lang frowned after her. "Why did you want to bring her onto your case so badly? She seems very abrasive. I wouldn't think jurors would like her."

"She's very smart," Brunelle answered. "And her abrasiveness complements my more charming demeanor."

He immediately regretted saying it that way.

"You do have a charming demeanor," Lang agreed, returning her bright-eyed gaze to him.

They stepped into the hallway and Brunelle tried to change the subject. He jabbed a thumb back at the courtroom where he had just arraigned Barnaby. "So, that's what I was so busy doing last night. Sorry I couldn't tell you. It was confidential, and a fluid situation. I was listening in and needed to be focused on those developments."

"No need to apologize, Dave," Lang replied. "I'm the one

who should apologize. I didn't expect to run into you, and I had had a little too much to drink when I saw you walk in. I should have realized you were busy and left you alone."

"Oh, well, no problem at all." Brunelle was relieved to accept her apology. "We've all been there. I know I have."

"Great," Lang said. "So, we're still on for next Saturday. I booked us a table at GlasHaus. I hear it's the fanciest restaurant in the city."

"Uh, wait, that is…" Brunelle stammered. "I thought you just said you'd had too much to drink."

"I had," Lang agreed, "but you made me a promise. I wasn't too drunk to forget that."

"Oh, okay, well." Brunelle rubbed the back of his neck. "It's just that, I was really more just trying to get you to let me focus on the case I was working on, and—"

"And you made me a promise," Lang repeated. "I asked you out and you said yes. Do you know how hard it is to get a reservation at GlasHaus? I had to pull some strings with some people I know down in Olympia, and even then I couldn't get us a table until nine p.m."

Brunelle did know how hard it was to get a reservation at GlasHaus. He had taken Casey there.

"Look, I just don't think this is a very good idea," Brunelle tried. "We're working together, in a way anyway, and I have a lot going on with this Grunwald case."

Lang crossed her arms and nodded as Brunelle tried to wriggle off her hook. "Anything else?"

"Uh, no, not really," Brunelle answered. "I just think maybe you should keep that reservation but go with somebody else."

Lang nodded again, then moved a half-step too close to

Brunelle. "Listen, Dave. I'm not an idiot. I'm a fucking auditor. I go into other people's jobs and see what they're doing wrong. I notice what people say, but even more than that I notice what they don't say. And in all the times you've tried to avoid going out with me, the one thing you've never told me is that you have a girlfriend. A girlfriend you live with, I might add."

Brunelle felt a dump of adrenaline at Lang's words, both that she knew about Casey and that she was right about what he hadn't said about her.

"You should think on that, Dave," Lang continued. "In the meantime, it's not my problem. You promised to have dinner with me, and I intend to hold you to that promise, or draw whatever reasonable conclusions I can from one of this office's supposedly top prosecutors not being a man of his word. As for what you tell your girlfriend, that's up to you."

Brunelle was at a loss for words as he imagined what he might possibly say to Casey about going to dinner with another woman.

"And Dave?" Lang continued. "After you tell her whatever you tell her, you should think on that too." She reached up and cupped his cheek in her hand. "See you next Saturday."

Brunelle watched her strut away down the long courthouse hallway. He knew he watched her too long.

CHAPTER 27

It took Edwards five days to review the police reports and contact Brunelle to confirm that she would have Barnaby give a proffer statement. It took two more to get everyone in the same room. Everyone meant Brunelle and Carlisle, Edwards and Barnaby, and Chen and Houser. Chen would be asking the questions; Houser was there for his technical expertise. Brunelle noted he seemed to be fanboying a bit at getting to meet The Owl.

In the week it took to put all of that together, Brunelle busied himself with other aspects of case preparation. Anything he could think of, really, even things that didn't actually need to be done or could, and maybe even should, wait until trial had actually begun. And in all that time, he didn't once mention to Casey anything about his dinner date with Lang. He also didn't cancel the date. He told himself he was just too busy to worry about it, let alone bring it up with Casey. But the problem with telling yourself something is that you know when you're lying.

"He better not lie to us again," Carlisle warned Edwards as everyone milled around the conference table to find their seats.

"What are you going to do, Gwen?" Edwards returned with a challenging grin. "Assault him again?"

Carlisle looked over at Barnaby, already seated and looking far too relaxed considering the circumstances. "I might."

"All right, all right," Brunelle stepped between them. "Enough of that. We have work to do. Everyone has a role. None of those roles include assaulting anyone."

Carlisle frowned at Brunelle, but didn't argue. Instead, she took a seat on the prosecution side of the table, next to where Brunelle would sit, Chen next to him, and Houser on the far side. They were lined up in the order most likely to whisper to the person next to them.

Edwards sat down next to Barnaby and opposite the others. "I've gone over the agreement with my client," she began. "He understands what he is doing today and what is expected of him, and he is eager to cooperate."

Brunelle doubted Barnaby was 'eager' to cooperate. He had been the opposite of eager to cooperate when Brunelle had chased him down on the mean streets of Fremont. But he was willing to cooperate and that was enough.

"Good. Then let's get started," Chen replied. He placed a portable audio recorder on the table between the two sides. "I will turn on the recording and we can go around the room. Everyone introduce themselves by name and title, and state that you consent to the audio recording."

Chen pressed the button and started the recitations. Brunelle wondered whether Barnaby would offer his title as 'The Owl,' but he opted for a more pedestrian label. "Aiden Barnaby. Software engineer."

"All right," Chen moved the gathering along. "Now I will advise Mr. Barnaby of certain warnings prior to providing his proffer statement. At the end I will ask him if he understands and agrees to the warnings. If he does, I will ask him and his attorney to sign at the bottom of the warning form, and we can begin the proffer. Is everyone in agreement with that procedure?"

Everyone was and said so.

Chen began reading from the form Barnaby would be signing. "I understand that I have the right to remain silent. I am choosing to provide a statement to law enforcement in the hope of receiving a more favorable resolution of my pending criminal charges. I have received no guarantees that I will receive such a more favorable resolution. Whether I receive a more favorable resolution will depend on the prosecuting attorney's assessment of my honesty in this statement and the usefulness of the statement for prosecution in another but related matter. I understand that anything I say during this statement cannot be used against me in my own criminal case, unless I testify in that case and provide information which is contrary to the information I provide in this statement. Understanding all this, and after consultation with my attorney, I hereby waive my right to remain silent and voluntarily provide a statement to law enforcement."

Chen looked up from the paper and at Barnaby. "Is that all true and accurate."

Barnaby nodded. "Yes, it is."

Chen slid the paper across the table. "Then you and Ms. Edwards sign that and we can get to the good stuff."

Brunelle exchanged a glance with Carlisle. They weren't entirely unnecessary to the proceedings, but if things went well, they could sit back and let Chen do all of the talking. All of the question asking anyway. Barnaby had some talking to do as well.

Edwards slid the signed warning form back to Chen, and

he began.

"Please state your name for the recording."

"Aiden Barnaby," he answered.

"How are you employed, Mr. Barnaby?" Chen continued.

"I am a software engineer with MegaThink."

Chen nodded. "Do you have any additional sources of income, whether reported or not on any official government documents?"

Brunelle knew Chen meant tax returns, but didn't want to spook Barnaby right out of the gate with a suggestion of federal tax fraud charges. That was outside of their jurisdiction; they couldn't offer immunity for federal crimes.

"I do have a side business," Barnaby acknowledged. "A side hustle, I guess is what people might call it."

"What is that side business?" Chen declined to label it a 'hustle,' much to Brunelle's unspoken approval.

"I write and sell bespoke computer programs," Barnaby answered. He didn't seem nervous at all. He was dressed comfortably in an open-collared dress shirt and slacks. Brunelle wished he were at least a little anxious. It would confirm he understood the seriousness of the situation.

Chen sighed slightly. Brunelle knew he didn't mind asking the questions, but he also knew Chen was irritated when he had to ask more than he should have to. "What sort of bespoke computer programs?"

"Well, that's just it," Barnaby answered. "They're bespoke. Specially designed for the needs of the buyer. I have written many different programs for many different buyers."

"Jess..." Brunelle spoke up in warning.

"He's just answering the questions honestly," Edwards defended. "Go ahead and get more specific. That will probably help."

Chen sighed again, but complied. "Have you ever written a program that permanently deletes files from a computer hard drive?"

Houser leaned over and whispered in Chen's ear.

"Rather than designate the files for possible overwriting?" Chen appended.

"Yes, I have," Barnaby admitted. "That sort of program is actually a frequent request from potential buyers." He pointed at Houser. "Like him, I thought."

That was awkward, but it wouldn't make sense on the recording anyway, so Brunelle let it slide. Chen and Houser did as well.

"Please explain how that program works," Chen pressed ahead.

So Barnaby did. It was basically the same explanation Houser had provided, except without the trash can prop.

"How often does the program purge the files?" Chen asked after the explanation. "Can we use the purge for what your program does?"

Barnaby nodded. "That's a bit blunt, but I suppose so."

"Great." Chen forced a polite smile. "How often does your program purge files?"

"It depends on what the buyer asks for," Barnaby answered, honestly if unhelpfully.

"Is it automatic," Chen followed up, "or do you have to run it manually every time you want to purge something?"

Barnaby shrugged. "Again, it depends on what the buyer asks for."

"Well, what did the buyer ask for in this case?" Chen demanded, betraying a growing frustration at the vagueness of the responses he was getting.

Brunelle interjected his own question before Barnaby answered. "And who was the buyer in this case? William Grunwald or Harrison Jacoby?"

Brunelle saw a smile unfurl across Edwards's face. She might be helping them in that moment, but she was also going to enjoy anything that wasn't helpful.

"I don't know," Barnaby answered. "They contacted me via chat room, just like he did." Another gesture toward Houser. "As for who picked it up and dropped off the money, I have no idea. I've never seen either of them, and I do not ask for I.D."

"Hold on." Brunelle had brought his paper case file with him. He flipped through it and removed two photographs: Grunwald's booking photo and a photo of Jacoby in his hospital bed. "Which of these two was it?"

He slid the photos across the table to Edwards. In turn, she moved them in front of her client. "It's okay if you can't remember," she advised. "It was a long time ago, it was dark, and you probably weren't trying to remember anyone's face."

"It wasn't that long ago," Brunelle spoke up. "It wasn't that dark. And I bet you make sure you get a good look at your buyer in case they're unhappy with your product and come looking for you."

Barnaby's eyes darted to Carlisle and back at the suggestion of someone doing him harm.

"Just do your best, Aiden," Edwards soothed. She threw a disapproving glare at Brunelle.

Barnaby looked at the photos for several moments, long enough to make Brunelle think he was actually trying to remember. The easier thing to do would have been to say he didn't recognize either of them, but apparently he took his promise to tell the truth seriously. At least in that moment.

"It wasn't this guy." He pushed Grunwald's booking photo away. He tapped on the picture of Jacoby in the ICU. "It's hard to say with this tube covering half his face, but I'm pretty sure it was this guy. He's the one who dropped off the money and took the program."

Brunelle was happy for the confirmation, but still wasn't sure what it meant.

"Did he say what they were going to use it for?" he went ahead and asked, ignoring Chen's irritated glance.

Barnaby shook his head. "Like I said, I don't ask that."

"What were the specs on the program?" Houser joined in taking the interview away from Chen. "Was it automatic or manual? If automatic, how often? Could it be loaded onto multiple machines? Does it erase itself after a certain amount of time? If not, where does it hide?"

Barnaby smiled at Houser. "Those are good questions. I can see why they had you try to trick me."

"Aw thanks," Houser replied.

"Just answer the questions," Brunelle barked.

Barnaby looked at him disapprovingly, but then did what he was told. "Manual. As often as they wanted. Yes. No. It loads itself into a dummy file in the driver's subdirectory."

Houser snapped his fingers. "Of course."

"So, it's still on the computer?" Carlisle jumped in to ask. Chen had completely lost control of the conversation anyway.

"Unless they deleted it," Barnaby said.

"Why would they do that?" Brunelle asked.

"Because they were done with it," Barnaby answered.

"Were they?" Carlisle wondered aloud.

"I'll find out," Houser replied. "Now that I know where

to look."

"Can we get back on track?" Chen finally spoke up. "I had a list of questions."

"Are you sure you don't already have the answers now?" Edwards suggested. "I'm not sure there's much more my client can tell you."

"And I would really like to get back to my lab and look at that laptop again," Houser added, practically bouncing in his chair.

"I have another question." Brunelle raised a finger.

Chen tossed his prepared questions aside. "Go ahead."

"Do you keep a backup somewhere of what's deleted?" Brunelle asked. "Like, does the program send you a copy before deleting it off the buyer's computer? It seems like that could be valuable information you could hold over someone's head, if things turned sour later."

Barnaby grinned and nodded. "That's very smart. And yes, I could do that. But I don't anymore. So, I know I didn't do that with this program."

"You said 'anymore,'" Brunelle noted. "So, you did that in the past. Why did you stop?"

"For one thing," Barnaby explained, "it's not smart to connect my computer to a buyer's computer. I mean, I know how to cover my tracks, but it's always better to have no tracks in the first place."

"What's the other thing?" Brunelle followed up.

Barnaby's grin faded. "I didn't like what I got sent."

Brunelle nodded. He could understand that. Everyone else in the room had signed up for a career that involved the close inspection of the worst things people did to each other. Barnaby was just a greedy software engineer with no morals.

"Anything else, then?" Edwards asked. "That's everything my client knows. I think it will help you in your case against Grunwald. If nothing else, it casts doubt on why they bought the program in the first place."

"Jacoby probably didn't buy it to delete emails instructing Grunwald to murder him," Brunelle agreed. "Yeah, we're done. For today. But part of this is he testifies at trial. He needs to tell the jury the same stuff he just told us."

Edwards looked to her client. "Are you willing to do that, Aiden?"

Barnaby shrugged. "What other choice do I have?"

Brunelle smiled. He knew Barnaby was smart.

CHAPTER 28

Brunelle beat Casey home that Friday night. He had ducked out a half hour early and the traffic on the I-90 bridge was lighter than usual. He didn't know why exactly, but he was glad for it. If nothing else, it would keep him from complaining to Casey about the traffic when she got home. He knew she took it to be a complaint about them living together. He didn't mean it that way, and she never said anything, but he could see it in her face sometimes.

So, he took the opportunity to start dinner. Nothing too fancy. Just some seasoned chicken breasts with rice and beans. And a fresh bottle of wine from the lower cupboard they jokingly referred to as their wine cellar. By the time Casey got home, Brunelle was out of his coat and tie, dinner was almost ready, and the wine was poured.

"Oh, Dave, you are a godsend," Casey kicked off her shoes and collapsed into his arms for a welcome home hug. "Today sucked. The chief called an impromptu meeting of all the detectives to have us update him on our cases. He's on some new data metrics kick. He went to a conference back East or something and now he wants to reduce all of our cases to spreadsheets. He's even talking about going back through the last ten years of closed cases to create a comparative data distribution field or something. I don't know. I didn't become a cop to do math."

Brunelle patted her back. "There, there. I don't like math either."

Casey ended the hug and stood back up straight. "I knew you'd understand." She looked into the kitchen. "And I knew you'd have the wine poured. White? So, is that chicken, I smell? It's not fish."

"It is chicken," Brunelle confirmed, "and it's almost done. Why don't you go change and I'll get it on the table?"

Casey gladly did as suggested and soon enough they were comfortable and eating at their dining room table.

"How was your day?" Casey asked. "Didn't you have something big today?"

"The proffer on the Grunwald case," Brunelle confirmed.

"How'd that go?" Casey asked before taking another sip of her wine. "Did he tell you what really happened?"

Brunelle shrugged and frowned slightly. "Not entirely. He doesn't actually know that. But what he does know is probably enough to convince the jury that Grunwald is lying."

"So, we still don't know Grunwald's motive, huh?" Casey lowered her fork and smiled at him. "That means I could still win the bet."

Brunelle knew to nod and agree. "You sure could. Although at this point, we might never know."

"What about the victim?" Casey asked. "Is there no way he's going to get better in time for the trial?"

"He might never get better," Brunelle answered. He was

glad he'd finished most of his meal. His appetite disappeared, replaced by a queasy sensation in the pit of his stomach. "I'm going to go to the hospital tomorrow night to talk to his doctor."

Casey frowned. "On a Saturday night? Why are you going then?"

Brunelle took another swig of wine, a vain attempt to quell the churn in his gut. "That's when the doctor is on shift."

"Oh," was all Casey said. She set her fork down and reached for her own wine glass.

"You know how doctors are," Brunelle continued. "They never answer the phone and they never call you back. I need to track him down in person and get an update on my victim's status. After Parmenter's ruling on the duress defense, whether Jacoby lives or dies actually may be the difference between winning and losing the case."

Casey nodded, but a frown tinted her lips. "That makes sense. Hopefully you won't have to work too late."

"I probably will," Brunelle replied. "His shift starts at nine. But just because he's on shift doesn't mean I'll find him right away, or that he'll be able or willing to talk to me when I do find him."

Casey hid her growing frown behind another drink of wine. "I guess I'm on my own tomorrow night."

Brunelle frowned too. "I guess so."

CHAPTER 29

Harborview Medical Center was all the way across town from the GlasHaus restaurant. Marietta Lang was going to be very disappointed at being stood up. But Brunelle really did need to talk with Jacoby's doctor, and he'd told Lang she should take someone else. Plus, it was none of Lang's damn business what he told Casey. He'd told her the truth. And if he was lucky enough to find Dr. Martinson right away, he might even be home again before Casey fell asleep in front of the television.

Jacoby was still in intensive care. As Brunelle rode the elevator to the ICU, he wondered how long a hospital would keep someone there before moving them to more of a hospice situation. Totally unrelated, Brunelle noted Grunwald's trial was scheduled to begin in two weeks.

The elevator opened with a ding that seemed awfully loud for the late hour. The rest of the floor was quiet, save the hum of machinery and the tapping at keyboards by the few staff working that night. Brunelle crossed the lobby to the central nurses' station and asked where he might be able to find Dr.

Kevin Martinson.

The nurse was a middle-aged woman with thick black curls and purple scrubs with ice cream cones printed on them. She raised an eyebrow at Brunelle's inquiry. "And you are?"

So, Brunelle explained. He wasn't dressed in a suit late on a Saturday night, but he had his court I.D. card on him that identified him as a prosecutor. That, combined with his specific knowledge of Dr. Martinson and his patient seemed to convince the nurse he was telling the truth.

"I'll page Dr. Martinson," she offered. "I don't know if he'll be able to respond right away. He's doing his rounds. He doesn't like being interrupted when he's talking with his patients."

Brunelle could admire that. It was looking like Casey would be falling asleep on the couch without him after all. He thanked the nurse and took a seat in the waiting area across the hall from the nurses' station. There was a television with some sort of nature documentary playing, but mercifully the sound was off. Brunelle could watch pictures of a rain forest if he chose to, without the fear of developing a headache from a too-loud T.V.

He took out his phone and considered texting Casey, but then thought better of it. He'd acted strangely enough at dinner the previous night. He didn't want to draw even more attention to his behavior by texting when he'd insisted he had to work. He hadn't done anything wrong. But he'd left the opportunity open too long, he knew.

He wondered what Lang was thinking, sitting alone at the table at GlasHaus. He wondered what she ordered. He wondered what she was wearing. Then he shook his head, pushed himself to his feet, and hurried back to the nurses' station.

"Could I maybe go see how Dr. Jacoby is doing myself," he asked, "while I'm waiting for Dr. Martinson?"

The nurse had no objection, other than to remind him of the protocols that applied to visiting an ICU patient. Brunelle thanked her yet again and made his way down the hallway. When he arrived, he again found Veronica Jacoby in the room. Only this time, she was curled up asleep on the large, vinyl-cushioned chair that had been pulled next to the bed. She was covered, barely, by a single thin hospital blanket. She looked cold, and exhausted, and to the extent a sleeping person could, she looked sad.

Brunelle stopped in the doorway. He didn't need to see Jacoby so badly that he wanted to risk waking Veronica up. For all he knew she had just fallen asleep after days at her husband's side.

He stepped backward, and directly into the lanky frame of Dr. Kevin Martinson.

"Oh! Sorry," Brunelle called out. Then, remembering the slumbering Veronica, he lowered his voice. "Sorry about that, doctor. Hey, do you happen to have a few minutes to talk with me again?"

Brunelle's hushed voice prompted Martinson to peer into the room. He spied Veronica as well and nodded. "Yes, but not here. Let's go to the waiting area."

Brunelle was fine with that so long as the nurses hadn't turned the television volume up. They had not, so Brunelle and Dr. Martinson were able to sit down and have a reasonably private conversation in the mostly deserted ICU.

"What can I help you with?" Martinson began. "Just looking for an update? As I recall, you said you didn't care whether Dr. Jacoby lived or died."

Brunelle frowned at that characterization of his words. "I said it didn't matter to my case," he protested, "but that has actually changed. Our judge made an unexpected ruling. Now, it could matter very much whether Dr. Jacoby survives. Is he going to?"

Martinson frowned. "There are limitations on what I can say, of course. Privacy laws and all that. Let me ask you a question. Is it better or worse for your case if he passes away?"

"Better," Brunelle admitted after a moment.

"Then I think you'll be pleased," Martinson said. "At least professionally."

Brunelle was not actually pleased to hear that. Not after seeing Veronica Jacoby curled up asleep next to her husband. Not after having that remind him of Casey curled up asleep, not next to him because he was working too late on a Saturday night.

"How long does he have?" Brunelle asked.

"How long do you have?" Martinson again answered a question with a question. "When is your trial?"

"Two weeks," Brunelle answered.

Martinson shook his head. "He'll still be alive in two weeks, I suspect. He's a fighter. So is his wife. She's basically moved in here. Honestly, I'm surprised he's doing as well as he is. Love can be very powerful."

Brunelle supposed that was probably true. He'd never given it the chance, he supposed. Or needed it to be.

"What happens if he dies after your trial?" the doctor asked.

"If the defendant is convicted of attempted murder," Brunelle explained, "we can increase the charges to completed murder if the victim dies within a year of the incident."

"And what if he's acquitted?" Martinson asked.

"If he's acquitted?" Brunelle shook his head. "If he's acquitted, then it won't matter one bit if Dr. Jacoby dies. We can't charge him with a murder a jury already said he didn't attempt to do."

"He'll get away with murder," Martinson translated. "No justice for Veronica."

"Exactly," Brunelle agreed.

He didn't like the news, but he needed to know it. He stood up and thanked the doctor for his time.

"If there's anything else I can do, please just let me know," Martinson made the mistake of saying.

Brunelle managed a grin despite the heavy atmosphere of the ICU. "There is one thing, doctor. I'll be serving you with a subpoena. I need you to explain to the jury what happened to Dr. Jacoby. And what's likely to happen to him after they make their decision."

CHAPTER 30

The last hearing before the trial began was called the Readiness Hearing, for obvious reasons. Judge Parmenter would ask the attorneys if they were ready for trial. The only thing that might lead an attorney to answer no to that question was additional information discovered on the eve of trial. That sort of thing would be good cause for a continuance of the trial date. That sort of thing was also what Brunelle was about to drop on Milliken.

"Mr. Brunelle. Ms. Carlisle." Milliken greeted the prosecutors when he and his client arrived in Judge Parmenter's courtroom for the Readiness. Grunwald did not join in the greeting. He sat down at the defense table and commenced extracting a legal pad and related items from a briefcase he had brought for himself. The courtroom was devoid of media or other spectators. Readiness was a quick and formal hearing. It was for the judge's benefit, not the public. Nothing newsworthy would occur.

"Nice to see you both again," Milliken said. "Perhaps I'll

get to hear Ms. Carlisle speak today. Or will I have to wait for the trial?"

"You'll know when I speak," Carlisle snarled at him.

Milliken just laughed. "Delightful. And we're both answering ready for trial?" he inquired. "I know I certainly am."

"About that..." Brunelle raised a cautionary finger. He reached into his own briefcase and extracted over an inch of papers. He pushed them toward Milliken. "This is new discovery. There's been a break in the case."

"A break in the case?" Milliken frowned, but he accepted the paperwork. "Has Dr. Jacoby passed away? Is this the autopsy report?"

"Uh, no," Brunelle answered. "No, he's still alive, although I don't know for how much longer."

"Oh good." Milliken slapped the papers in his hand. "Then whatever this is, I can deal with it. We are ready for trial."

"Don't you even want to know what it is?" Carlisle asked.

"Of course I do, Ms. Carlisle," Milliken answered, "but as I'm sure you're aware, I'm in a bit of a race against time here. Judge Parmenter has graciously, and correctly, ruled that I may present our duress defense to the jury. That ruling was dependent on this being an attempted murder case, and not a completed murder case. The moment Dr. Jacoby dies, and it is my understanding that that is now the expected outcome, I lose that defense. So, you see, no matter what this is," he held the papers up slightly, "it would be malpractice for me to seek a continuance of the trial date. I will simply have to deal with this, whatever it is." He looked again at the stack of reports. "What is it?"

"We found the guy who sold your client the computer file deletion program," Brunelle answered. "It wasn't for deleting emails from the dark web or whatever your guy was planning on telling the jury."

Milliken kept an expressionless poker face. "That is a development. Under different circumstances, I would request a continuance. Now, I'll just have to review this and decide between two other options."

"What are those?" Carlisle asked.

"Moving to suppress them from evidence for some basis I will think of later," Milliken explained, "or allowing them in and using them against you to prove my client acted under duress after all."

Brunelle didn't have a snappy comeback for that. Carlisle remained quiet as well. Everyone had said what needed to be said. It was time to wait for the judge. Milliken sat down next to his client. Brunelle and Carlisle sat down at the prosecution table. And within minutes of being so seated, they were all called to their feet again by the bailiff.

"All rise! The King County Superior Court is now in session, the Honorable Andrew Parmenter presiding."

"Please be seated," Parmenter instructed. "Are the parties ready on the matter of *The State of Washington versus William Grunwald*?"

"The State is ready, Your Honor," Brunelle answered. Milliken would have to wait for the trial to hear Carlisle address the Court.

"The defense is ready as well, Your Honor," Milliken added.

"Excellent," Judge Parmenter replied. "We are assembled today for the Readiness Hearing. Trial is scheduled to commence in one week. So, I will inquire first of the prosecution. Is the State ready for trial?"

"Yes, Your Honor," Brunelle answered.

"Any outstanding issues on your end, Mr. Brunelle?" Parmenter inquired.

Brunelle glanced over at the last bit of discovery he had just provided the defense. "Not anymore, Your Honor. No."

Parmenter frowned slightly at Brunelle's response, but did not inquire further. Instead, he turned to the defense table. "And is the defendant ready for trial, Mr. Milliken?"

Brunelle wondered whether Milliken might try to make a record of having just received new reports. But he simply flashed a broad smile at the judge and answered, "The defense is ready, Your Honor."

"Excellent," Judge Parmenter repeated. "Then I will excuse the parties, with instructions to return to my courtroom exactly one week from today. We will begin punctually at nine a.m. Do not be late."

Brunelle and Milliken both assured the judge they would be on time, and then the Readiness Hearing was complete. The judge departed the courtroom, followed closely by the bailiff and court reporter. In short order, only the lawyers and Grunwald remained.

"I'm surprised," Brunelle said to Milliken, "you didn't at least make a record of the last-minute discovery we gave you this morning. That could make a good appeal issue."

"Appeal?" Milliken laughed. "Oh no, Mr. Brunelle. Appeals are for the losing side. I very much intend to win this case."

CHAPTER 31

Six days and eight hours later it was the night before trial, a time Brunelle had historically set aside for mandatory rest and quiet reflection. He would need his body and mind in top condition the next morning, and nothing served that better than an ounce of whiskey, a view of the skyline, and an early bedtime.

But that was when he was single and lived in Seattle.

He could salvage the ounce of whiskey, but thoughtful solitude and extra sleep were no longer on the schedule. And the view was the wooden fence between their backyard and the neighbor's. There were also a couple of evergreen trees in one corner.

"Here you are." Casey stepped out onto the back porch and handed Brunelle that shot of whiskey. She had one for herself as well. "So, big day tomorrow, huh?"

Brunelle accepted the glass. "Yup."

Casey sat down next to him. "Did you ever figure out the motive?"

Brunelle took a sip of whiskey and shook his head. "No. If anything, I know less about Grunwald's motive now than I did when the case started. I just know he's lying. I'm back to my original plan: telling the jury I don't have to prove motive."

"I still hate that plan," Casey replied.

"Yeah, I don't like it much anymore either," Brunelle agreed. "I really thought we'd find something when we nabbed that owl guy, but it just made everything even less clear. Why would Jacoby buy the deletion program?"

"Figure that out," Casey tipped her glass at him, "and you win the case."

Brunelle sighed. "I have to win the case a different way, because I don't think I'm going to get an answer to that question. The only two people who know are in a coma and on trial. One can't tell the truth and the other won't. I'll be stuck with whatever Grunwald claims on the stand. I'll just have to try to poke enough holes in it that it collapses."

"And we'll never know the real reason he shot his business partner," Casey concluded.

"Nope," Brunelle agreed.

A long silence ensued as Brunelle thought more about the case, and Casey thought about something else.

"So, I guess I lose the bet," she said finally, eyes fixed firmly on that wooden fence across the yard. Their yard.

Brunelle took another sip of whiskey. He reached over and put his hand on hers. "You never know what will happen once a trial starts. By the end of it we could be picking out wedding cakes."

Casey laughed. "That's how I always imagined it happening. Thanks, honey."

She turned her hand over and laced her fingers through his. But she kept her gaze distant.

CHAPTER 32

The media was back for the first day of trial. They were going to be disappointed, Brunelle knew. They had come for opening statements, witness testimony, cross-examination. None of that would be happening for days. There were preliminary matters to be handled before the drama of the actual trial began to unfold. Things like scheduling, seating, and preliminary motions regarding routine evidence issues which didn't merit lengthy contested hearings but needed to be addressed just the same. And there was the biggest task to be completed before the lawyers could stand up to deliver their opening statements: selecting the jurors to listen to those opening statements and everything else that would follow. Only once all of that was done should the cameras return.

There wasn't even any trash talk between the attorneys that first morning. It was hard to get worked up over whether the morning break should be from 10:00-10:15 or 10:15-10:30.

"Good morning, counsel," Milliken greeted Brunelle and Carlisle when he arrived in Parmenter's courtroom shortly before the judge was scheduled to take the bench. "Lovely day to start a trial, don't you think?"

Brunelle was agnostic on the matter. He may not have been up for trash talk, but he wasn't a big fan of small talk either.

"If you say so," Carlisle answered for them both.

Milliken accepted the curt reply with a small nod and a half-smile. Then he joined his client who had once again already sat down at the defense table. Grunwald was the star of the show, the reason all of them, including the media—especially the media—were there, yet he would say not one word above a whisper into his lawyer's ear until and unless he took the stand in several weeks' time.

Brunelle knew it was more 'until' than 'unless,' but as he'd said to Casey the night before, anything could happen once the trial started. If the prosecution case was the one that collapsed, Grunwald might never need to take the stand. But that was a long way away. First they needed to decide whether to end the day at 4:30 or 4:45.

"All rise! The King County Superior Court is now in session, The Honorable Andrew Parmenter presiding."

The judge emerged from his chambers and took his seat above the courtroom. "Please be seated. Are the parties ready to begin the trial in the matter of *The State of Washington versus William Grunwald*?"

Brunelle, who had remained standing in anticipation of that very question, answered first. "The State is ready, Your Honor."

Milliken stood up again. "The defense is ready as well, Your Honor."

And they were off. In the way the coin toss began a football game or the pit orchestra warming up began the opera. It wasn't nothing, but it wasn't much more than that either.

Brunelle and Carlisle took turns addressing the various issues to be ironed out. It was good for both of them to stretch their legs, so to speak, and it was good for Parmenter to get used to hearing from both of them and see them acting as a team. The scheduling and basic evidentiary issues took almost all of the first day to address. They came back the second day to begin the process of jury selection. The media did not come back the second day. In fact, they left as soon as that scheduling portion established when opening statements would be.

They needed to seat twelve jurors, plus at least two alternate jurors in the event one of the regular jurors was unable to continue halfway through the trial. That happened more often than one might think, and would result in a mistrial if there wasn't someone to step in immediately so the trial could continue. Parmenter suggested four alternates because of a series of misfortunes in his last trial. Neither Brunelle nor Milliken objected. Anything that reduced the risk of a mistrial and having to start the trial over was a good thing. Brunelle had to fight against the urge to want a mistrial and restart in the morbid hope that Jacoby might die if he could drag things out long enough. He would hardly be championing justice for the victim if he wished him death.

The process for seating sixteen total jurors was to bring in a hundred potential jurors, then whittle away at the ones who one side or the other, or the judge, thought should not be in the final jury. Each side was allowed to strike six potential jurors for no reason other than feeling like they would be too sympathetic to the other side. In addition, the judge would excuse any juror who had a good reason they couldn't sit on a weeks-long trial. Such reasons included financial hardship from missing so much work, prepaid vacation plans, or any philosophical reason they would be unable to follow the law in the particular case. That could be a problem when asking twelve Seattleites to convict a defendant for possessing drugs most of them thought should be legal. But Brunelle had yet to meet a potential juror who wanted to legalize murder, or the attempt of it.

Those hundred people would be numbered and the first twelve would be the presumptive jury, with the next four the presumptive alternates. The lawyers and the judges would then talk to them, all of them, to learn what they could about those hardships and sympathies and biases. That took days. Finally, the striking would commence. First, the judge would excuse those who couldn't serve. Then, the lawyers would take turns excusing the ones they didn't want to serve. At the end, there were sixteen men and women seated in the jury box who raised their right hands and promised the judge they would, "Well and truly decide the case before them."

Then, everyone went home for a good night's rest. The next morning, the jury box and the courtroom were packed again. Not only had the media returned, but so had those junior prosecutors and defense attorneys who wanted to learn from watching a pair of the old guard clash. Also present were the people with the greatest interest in the outcome. Elizabeth Grunwald sat in the first row behind her husband. Veronica Jacoby, looking no less exhausted than the last time Brunelle had seen her, took a seat directly behind him and Carlisle.

Once everyone was assembled, Judge Parmenter took the bench and addressed the jurors.

"Ladies and gentlemen of the jury, please give your attention to Mr. Brunelle, who will deliver the opening statement on behalf of The State of Washington."

CHAPTER 33

Brunelle stood up and buttoned his suit coat. He stepped out from behind the prosecutors' counsel table and walked across the well between the judge's bench and the jury box. Then he took up the same spot in front of the jury that he delivered all of his closing arguments from. Dead center, three steps back. Close enough to command attention. Any closer and it would invade the jurors' space. Any farther away and it would communicate a lack of confidence in his case. And he needed to remain confident about their case.

He and Carlisle had divvied up the case. They would each do half the witnesses, and they split opening statement and closing argument. Carlisle would do an excellent job in closing, pulling all the evidence together to show the jury how they had met their burden to prove the charge beyond a reasonable doubt. But that wasn't why she was doing the closing argument. She was doing it because Brunelle wanted to do the opening statement.

There was something almost magical about the anticipation that filled a courtroom when a prosecutor stood up to deliver the opening statement. At the beginning of jury selection, when the one hundred jurors were brought into the courtroom, the judge told them that it was a criminal case and what the charge was; but he didn't tell them any of the facts. The lawyers weren't allowed to get into the facts either. They danced around them with questions about fairness, and business partnerships, and computer programming. The jurors knew the defendant must have done something to be sitting in that chair, but they were also told that they had to presume he was totally innocent. They were dying to know what had happened. And the first time anyone was finally allowed to sate that ever-growing curiosity was when the prosecutor finally stood up and told them why they were all there.

"The defendant, Dr. William Grunwald, pressed a loaded nine millimeter handgun against the skull of his longtime friend and business partner, Dr. Harrison Jacoby," Brunelle began. "And then he pulled the trigger."

That really should have been the end of it. That was attempted murder, no ifs ands or buts. But lawyers made their money in the ifs ands or buts, and Milliken knew how to make a lot of money.

"There is no question that this happened," Brunelle continued. "There are only two questions left. One, will Dr. Jacoby live or die? You see, Dr. Jacoby flinched and the defendant faltered, and his shot failed to fully penetrate his victim's skull. Instead, Dr. Jacoby suffered a massive brain bleed and lays unconscious even now in the intensive care unit of Harborview Medical Center. He is still alive, albeit barely, and no thanks to William Grunwald."

Brunelle paused just long enough to shift his weight and raise two fingers. "The second question is, why would the defendant do this? Why would he try to murder his business partner? A man he had been friends with for two decades? They had helped each other become successful. They had helped each other become rich. The defendant had a life anyone would envy. He had everything anyone could ever want. But apparently it wasn't enough. He made a decision to try to kill his friend and partner. We may never know the exact reasons why, but ultimately those reasons don't matter."

Brunelle had no choice but to lean into his original assessment of the case. "We may not be able to prove what the defendant's motive was, but we also don't have to. Motive is not an element of the crime of attempted murder. Would I like to know why he did that terrible, depraved thing? Would you like to know? Of course. But do you need to know before you can return a verdict of guilty? Absolutely not."

One of the problems with the law is that it was developed and clarified by lawyers, and lawyers could lose sight of common sense. The idea that a jury could convict a defendant of a crime without knowing why he did it was ludicrous on its face, and yet that was the law. At the end of the trial, the judge would tell them they had to accept the law as he instructed them, regardless of what they thought the law was or ought to be. But the reason the judge would tell them that was because they would very much want to do the opposite. They would want to know the defendant's motive in order to feel comfortable in the conclusion that he committed the crime. That was just common sense. But it wasn't the law.

So, Brunelle needed to reassure them.

"Now, that being said, I understand you will want to know what could drive a successful plastic surgeon and businessman like Dr. William Grunwald to try to murder his partner. And I can tell you that after you hear all of the evidence in the case, you will not only be convinced that he did it, you will be able to feel confident as to why he did it, even if it was something as simple as, as base as, just money. Most premeditated crimes are committed because of money or love. And there is nothing special about William Grunwald or what he did that fateful night."

It was important to knock the defendant down a peg or two over the course of the trial. Especially when the defendant was someone whose social and financial position would normally put him above everyone, including the government lawyer trying to put him in prison for a few decades. Everyone in that courtroom was there because of what Grunwald did. He was undeniably the most important person in the room. But that didn't mean he was the best person in the room. Something else to remind the jury of.

"So, what happened exactly?" Brunelle continued. "Well, the best way to share the story might be to tell it from the viewpoint of the hard working first responders who managed to save Harrison Jacoby's life, notwithstanding the intentions and actions of the defendant."

That was probably not the best way to tell the story, actually, but it was the only way Brunelle could tell it. It was how he would put on his case.

"Shortly before one o'clock in the morning," he began, "9-1-1 dispatch received a call. The caller was the defendant, William Grunwald. He reported that his friend and partner, Dr. Harrison Jacoby, had been shot and killed at their place of business. Now, did he tell the 9-1-1 operator that he was the shooter? No, he did not. He made up a story about a robbery. Not surprising perhaps, but important. Because when police arrived, the defendant opened the door of his business with the attempted murder weapon in his hand. And it was only then that he first admitted to pulling the trigger. And it would be even later that he offered an excuse to the police. But," he raised his hand, "I'm getting ahead of myself."

He shifted his weight again and allowed himself one small step to the left. Generally, he kept his feet rooted to the ground, to avoid the rookie trial attorney mistake of pacing in front of the jury. But there were times when a well-timed step or two to one side could communicate confidence or sincerity. There was no inherent problem with moving while speaking to the jury. The problem was doing so other than intentionally.

"Police immediately disarmed the defendant," Brunelle continued, then went inside the business to see if they could render aid to the victim. A bit to their surprise, they could. Dr. Jacoby was not dead, despite being shot in the head by the defendant. The police officers administered CPR and called for medical aid. Paramedics arrived and took over life support efforts. They transported Dr. Jacoby to Harborview where, despite the best efforts of the defendant, they saved Dr. Jacoby's life. He was in a coma, but he was alive. And that is exactly the same status he is in today." Brunelle pointed out the window in the general direction of the hill above downtown. "In the ICU at Harborview. In a coma. Barely alive. No thanks to the defendant."

Brunelle had made a point of dropping 'Doctor' when referring to Grunwald, opting instead for defendant most of the time, but keeping the honorific when referring to Jacoby. He needed to keep it subtle enough that the jurors wouldn't think it disrespectful, but consistent enough that it would unconsciously lower Grunwald in the jurors' eyes. Not only was every movement in closing argument important, every word mattered as well.

"The defendant admitted that he had lied to 9-1-1 and was the one who shot Dr. Jacoby," Brunelle continued his story. "He was placed under arrest and detained for questioning. That questioning was conducted by Seattle Police Detective Larry Chen. But it took some time for Detective Chen to arrive. Time for the defendant to come up with a new story. That robbery tale wasn't going to cut it."

Brunelle paused long enough to offer the jury a weary half-smile. "You know, you do this job long enough and you realize there are really only two defenses to most crimes. I didn't do it, or I had to do it. The defendant wasn't going to be able to claim he didn't do it. The gun was in his hand. So, he was left with, 'I had to do it.' And when Detective Chen arrived and questioned him, the defendant admitted to shooting his business partner in the head, but he claimed he had no choice."

Another pause to allow the jurors to begin speculating about what the details of that claim might be. Then Brunelle joined them.

"Did the defendant claim self-defense, the most common version of the 'I had to do it' defense? No. It's hard to claim self-defense when you shoot a man in the back of his head. What about defense of others? Was someone else in danger and the defendant had to stop Dr. Jacoby from harming them? No. It was one o'clock in the morning. No one else was there. Necessity? I had to shoot him to stop him from doing something even worse? No. Again, there was no one else there. What harm could Dr. Jacoby possibly have perpetrated? That left only one possible defense to cling to. Duress. The 'devil made me do it' defense. Someone else forced him to do it."

Brunelle paused to assess the jurors. Most of them were trying hard to show no reaction to his presentation, but a few were less circumspect of their expressions, and those few seemed appropriately skeptical of the duress defense that Brunelle was able, by virtue of the prosecutor always speaking to the jurors first, to frame in a negative way.

"Who? you might ask. Who could force a successful plastic surgeon, businessman, husband, and father to throw everything away in order to try to kill someone he had no apparent quarrel with? And you could be excused to think no one could do that, because even the defendant couldn't think of anyone. So, he made up someone the police could never confirm or dispel. He claimed he received anonymous emails from an unknown source who threatened to harm his son unless he killed Dr. Jacoby, and without explaining why they wanted Dr. Jacoby dead."

Another pause to make sure the jurors seemed to think that as incredible as Brunelle did.

"Detective Chen was understandably doubtful of the claim, but asked the defendant to see the emails. But of course there were no emails. He had deleted them all, on orders of the nameless blackmailers. But," Brunelle raised a finger again and stepped back to his original position in front of the center of the jury box, "this is where it gets interesting."

As if shooting a man in the head wasn't interesting enough, Brunelle thought to himself.

"You're going to hear testimony from Detective Jack Houser of the Seattle Police Department. Detective Houser is an expert in computer technology. He's going to explain to you that when you delete a file from your computer, whether it's an email or a spreadsheet or a letter to your mother, that file doesn't actually disappear from your computer. Instead it's moved to a different folder and made eligible to be overwritten. If the computer needs memory to save a new email or spreadsheet or letter to your mother than it can write over the supposedly deleted emails. So, those emails the defendant claimed he deleted should still have been on his laptop. But they weren't. Because they never existed in the first place."

That was the argument, Brunelle realized. It wasn't that The Owl's program deleted Grunwald's emails but no one knew why Jacoby was the one who bought the program. It was that Jacoby bought it for a different reason and Grunwald knew about it and latched onto it as his explanation of why there were no emails.

But Brunelle didn't want to spend a lot of time on The Owl in his opening statement.

"You're also going to hear from a local computer programmer who sells software that can truly purge files from your computer, not just set them aside to be discovered later by an expert like Detective Houser. This programmer goes by the street name 'The Owl' and he's going to tell you that he did sell a program like that to a partner in Grunwald and Jacoby, cosmetic surgeons. Only it wasn't to the defendant. It was to Dr. Jacoby."

Brunelle took another moment. He was nearing the end of his opening statement, if only because he was also reaching the end of the facts he knew about the case. It was time to wrap it up.

"So, ladies and gentlemen of the jury, I ask you to pay close attention to the evidence produced in this case. And if you do that you will be convinced beyond a reasonable doubt that the defendant shot Dr. Harrison Jacoby in the head, that he did so with the intent to kill Dr. Jacoby, and that his claims of acting under duress are nothing more than a transparent and legally inadequate attempt to avoid responsibility for his actions. Thank you."

Brunelle offered the slightest nod to the jurors, then walked briskly back to his chair and sat down.

"How was it?" he asked Carlisle out of the corner of his mouth even as he kept his eyes on the jurors.

"Solid B," Carlisle replied. "Maybe B-plus."

He knew she was teasing him, but they both knew he couldn't react in front of the jurors. "Fuck you," he whispered at her. There was no time for any further discussion

"And now, ladies and gentlemen," Judge Parmenter boomed, "please give your attention to Mr. Milliken, who will deliver the opening statement on behalf of the defendant."

CHAPTER 34

All eyes turned to Derek Milliken. He obviously knew it. And even more obviously, he loved it. He stood and slowly walked out from behind the defendant's table, a finger trailing atop it as he broke away and took his place in front of the jury box. It was almost the exact same spot Brunelle had stood in, but a half step closer and even less to one side. He avoided taking up the expected position.

"A bit to my surprise," he began with a velvety tone he had reserved even from his argument to the judge about bail and his duress defense, "and I'm sure to your surprise as well, I mostly agree with the prosecutor."

He turned and offered what seemed to be a congratulatory nod to Brunelle.

"Mr. Brunelle's recitation of the facts in this case were excellent," Milliken continued. "I couldn't have done better myself. Well, maybe I could have, but I don't need to. Everything he said about what happened is absolutely accurate. My client did shoot his longtime friend and business partner, Dr. Harrison

Jacoby. He did call 9-1-1 and initially report a robbery. Then when the police arrived, he provided the police the attempted murder weapon and confessed to what he had done. The evidence on all of these facts will be direct and uncontested. We agree on what Dr. Grunwald did. The disagreement, the entire crux of this case, is not what he did, but why."

Another look back at Brunelle, but with a frown rather than a nod. "In their zeal for a conviction, the prosecutors implore you to ignore Dr. Grunwald's explanation of why he acted as he did, while at the same time asking you to believe everything else he said about what happened. Believe the what and how, they ask you, but ignore the why."

Milliken lowered his eyes and shook his head. "Well, that's not how it works, ladies and gentlemen. That's certainly not how it should work. Listen to Dr. Grunwald, but listen to everything he has to say, and you will understand why he did what he did. And, more importantly perhaps, is the fact that the law also understands why he did what he did. When a person commits a criminal act while under duress, it is a complete defense to the crime committed. And so while Mr. Brunelle told you that it doesn't matter why Dr. Grunwald did what he did, the truth is that the law cares the absolute most about why he did it. Because if he did it under duress, it may be a tragedy, but it is not a crime."

Milliken paused for a moment, mostly to signal a slight change in topic. The jurors had been passively listening to lawyers drone on for some time already. As a career defense attorney, Milliken would be aware of making his point before fatigue caused the jurors to stop listening to him, or worse, disliking him. He needed to tell the jury what he would give them, why it mattered, then sit down again.

"Dr. Grunwald will testify in this trial," Milliken started up again. "He will tell you the same thing he told the police on the very night of the shooting. In the weeks prior to the incident, he was unexpectedly contacted by an unknown person or persons who had a personal, but secret vendetta, against his friend and partner, Dr. Jacoby. They wanted Dr. Grunwald to murder his friend, which, of course, he would never agree to do. But then they showed him proof that they had been stalking Dr. Grunwald's family, and they threatened the safety and life of his only child if he didn't do what they said. Dr. Grunwald didn't want to hurt Dr. Jacoby, but he had to protect his own son first. He did what they said, and even followed their direction to tell the authorities it was a burglary gone wrong."

Milliken paused again and looked sympathetically at his client, who sat up straight with his hands steepled in front of him and a grateful expression on his face as he listened to his attorney defend his honor. Brunelle thought all he was missing was a crooked halo over his head.

"But when the police arrived," Milliken turned back to the jury, "he told them the truth. He had shot Dr. Jacoby. And he had been forced to do it to protect his own family."

Milliken clasped his hands in front of himself, a gesture of sincerity all trial attorneys learned to mimic.

"The prosecution is going to go down a rabbit hole about computer programs and deleted files and a bunch of stuff that neither I nor Dr. Grunwald really understand. The blackmailers instructed him to delete their emails and he did so. Why Detective Houser wasn't able to find them, I can't say. Perhaps if he were that good with computers, he wouldn't have to work for the government."

Brunelle raised his hands slightly at the insult, then

caught himself and lowered his hands again.

"In any event," Milliken went on, "I urge you to listen to what Dr. Grunwald knows and ignore what the police and prosecution are guessing now. And if you do that, you will understand two things. First, that Dr. Grunwald was acting under duress. And second, that under the law, he is not guilty of the crime of attempted murder. Thank you."

Milliken offered another small bow of his head, then made his way back to his seat. Opening statements were over. It was time to get to the evidence.

Judge Parmenter looked down at the prosecution table. "The State may call its first witness."

It was Carlisle's turn. She stood up and announced, "The State calls Veronica Jacoby to the stand."

CHAPTER 35

Veronica Jacoby stood up from her seat in the front row and stepped forward into the well. Carlisle directed her to the judge who instructed her to raise her right hand.

"Do you solemnly swear or affirm," Parmenter put to her, "that your testimony will be the truth, the whole truth, and nothing but the truth?"

"Yes, Your Honor," Veronica confirmed.

"Please take your seat on the witness stand," the judge directed. Then, to Carlisle, "Whenever you're ready, counsel."

Carlisle took up a spot next to the jury box, at the end farthest from the witness stand. It was an old trick to encourage the witness to deliver their answers to the jury, which jurors loved, and also to make sure the witness kept their voice up. If the lawyer at the end of the jury box couldn't hear the witness, then neither could those farthest jurors. And there was something about the pressure of testifying in front of a room full of strangers that led some people to lose the strength in their voice.

"Please state your name for the record," Carlisle began.

"Veronica Jacoby," she answered, quietly but not too quietly.

"Good morning, Ms. Jacoby," Carlisle said. "I'd like to ask you a few questions about your husband. Is that okay?"

Of course it's okay, Brunelle knew. They had subpoenaed Veronica. She had no choice but to answer their questions. But Carlisle used the exchange to communicate, not with Veronica, but to the jury that this was serious business and Veronica was traumatized by the actions of the defendant.

"Yes," Veronica answered after a moment's hesitation. "That's why I'm here."

"Indeed," Carlisle agreed. "Let's get right to it then, shall we? Do you know someone named Harrison Jacoby?"

"Yes," Veronica answered. "He's my husband."

"And do you know William Grunwald," Carlisle asked, "the defendant in this case?"

Veronica nodded and her mouth tightened into a straight line. She avoided looking at Grunwald as he sat across the room from her. "Yes."

"How do you know Dr. Grunwald?" Carlisle continued.

"He's my husband's business partner," Veronica answered. "Or he was. Maybe he still is. I don't know. I thought that mattered at first, but it doesn't matter. It doesn't matter at all."

Carlisle allowed that answer to sink in with the jury, then followed up on it. "Why doesn't it matter?"

"Because Harry is in a coma," Veronica sobbed. "He's probably going to die. And it's all Bill's fault."

Carlisle waited a moment to give space to Veronica's emotions. "And Bill is the defendant, William Grunwald?"

"Yes." Veronica waved a perturbed hand. "Bill. William.

He shot Harry. He shot him in the head for no reason at all."

Carlisle nodded. "Now, to be clear, you weren't present when this happened, is that correct?"

Milliken could have objected to Veronica's assertion that Grunwald shot her husband. She didn't see it, so it was hearsay. But Milliken himself had told the jury Grunwald had shot Jacoby. It would have been pedantic at best to object to Veronica's testimony on that fact.

"That's correct," Veronica confirmed. "I was informed later by the police. And then, of course, your office filed charges against Bill."

"We did." Carlisle nodded. "Let's talk a little bit about the time leading up to your husband being shot. Do you recall him acting different in any way in the weeks leading up to the shooting?"

"He was working a little more," Veronica answered. "Some late nights here and there. But other than that, everything was fine. Better than ever, actually. With the extra hours he was putting in, it seemed like we had more money. We were planning a trip to Bali."

"Did your husband ever mention any difficulties with Dr. Grunwald?" Carlisle continued. "Were they having disagreements at work? Was there some new problem between them or anything like that?"

Veronica shook her head. "No, nothing like that." She paused. "I mean, nothing he told me about anyway. I didn't always like to hear about his work constantly, but I think he would have told me if he and Bill were having some sort of disagreement."

"So, when the police told you Dr. Grunwald had tried to murder your husband," Carlisle summarized, "were you surprised by that?"

"I was in shock," Veronica answered.

"What about now?" Carlisle asked. "Do you know now why Dr. Grunwald would have tried to kill your husband?"

Veronica looked at Grunwald then. A cold, pained look. "I still don't know why he did it. I wish I did. It might make it easier."

"Make what easier?" Carlisle asked.

Veronica's expression fell and her proud shoulders dropped. "Accepting that Harry is gone." The tip of her nose was turning red as she tried not to cry. Brunelle could see the dark bags under her eyes shining through her makeup. "I mean, he's not dead—not yet anyway—but he's in a coma, and the doctors say he'll probably never come out of it." She dropped her head into her hands and choked back a sob. "I lost my best friend," she croaked, "and I don't know why."

Brunelle looked to Carlisle, who threw a knowing glance back at him. A huge part of trial work was knowing when to sit down.

"Thank you, Mrs. Jacoby," Carlisle said. "No further questions."

Carlisle walked back to the prosecution table, but Veronica wasn't done yet.

"Any cross-examination, Mr. Milliken?" Judge Parmenter invited.

Milliken stood to address the judge. He looked at Veronica who was fighting back tears, then at the jurors who were likely sympathetic to her, then back to Parmenter who was waiting.

"Just two questions, Your Honor," Milliken answered. The precision of his response focused everyone's attention even more on him. He didn't conceal his pleasure at that.

He walked out from behind the defense table and took a neutral position halfway between the table and the witness stand.

"So, to the best of your knowledge and belief," he asked Veronica, "there were absolutely no problems, issues, bad feelings, or anything of the like between Dr. Jacoby and Dr. Grunwald, is that correct?"

Veronica nodded. "That's correct."

Milliken smiled. "And so, you would agree with me that there must have been some other, outside influence that caused Dr. Grunwald to do what he did, would you not?"

"Objection," Carlisle interrupted. "Calls for speculation."

It certainly did that. Milliken didn't argue the point, and Parmenter sustained the objection. But the jury heard the question, which was what Milliken really wanted.

"No further questions, Your Honor," he announced and returned to his seat.

Judge Parmenter looked down at the prosecution table. "Any redirect-examination, Ms. Carlisle?"

She looked to Brunelle for confirmation and he offered it with a small shake of his head.

"No, Your Honor," Carlisle answered.

"Thank you, Mrs. Jacoby," Judge Parmenter turned to address the witness. "You are excused from further testimony."

Veronica could only muster a nod in acknowledgement and thanks. Brunelle expected her to return to her seat behind them, but instead she hurried out of the courtroom, a hand over her face.

Perfect, Brunelle thought. He hoped the jurors saw it too.

"And now, ladies and gentlemen of the jury," Judge Parmenter announced, "it is time for our morning recess. The trial will recommence in fifteen minutes."

The bailiff called for everyone to rise at the judge's departure. The people in the gallery began muttering and moving about and muttering, most trying to decide if there was enough time to bother trying to use the bathroom.

"So far, so good," Carlisle offered her appraisal to Brunelle.

"Agreed," Brunelle replied. "She did good. But we have a long way to go still."

Carlisle nodded. "No need to tell me. I have half the witnesses. It's going to take weeks to put on our case."

"Yep." Brunelle glared over at Grunwald, crouched over and whispering to Milliken. "And at the end of it, we still won't really know why he did it."

CHAPTER 36

The next witnesses were the professionals. The patrol officers who responded. The paramedics who treated Jacoby. The forensics officers who documented the scene. All of them were important to tell the jury the full story of what happened. None of them had any insight on why.

Despite their lack of information on that crucial point, they had plenty of information on everything else, and there were a lot of them. If Brunelle and Carlisle failed to call any of them to the stand, Milliken would be able to argue that they did so intentionally because they feared the witness would say something favorable to the defense. That meant several days of technical witnesses, recounting technical details, and being subject to little to no cross-examination. By the time the first week of trial was in the books, Brunelle and Carlisle had examined a dozen witnesses and Milliken had asked less than a dozen questions.

The following Monday marked week two of the trial, and Brunelle celebrated the landmark by calling a witness Milliken would be hard pressed not to cross-examine at least a little bit.

"The State calls Dr. Kevin Martinson to the stand," he announced.

Martinson strode into the courtroom looking every bit the competent medical professional. He wore a dark gray suit with white shirt and blue tie. His gait was quick and his eyes sharp. Judge Parmenter swore him in and a moment later he was seated in the witness stand, leaning forward slightly and ready to answer the questions put to him.

When they were dividing up the witnesses, Brunelle thought it best if he did the direct examination of Martinson. They had already spoken twice, so they had established a rapport. Plus, it let him push a less interesting witness or two onto Carlisle's plate.

"Could you please state your name for the record?" Brunelle began. He too stood next to the far end of the jury box, but the jurors would have no trouble hearing Dr. Martinson.

"Kevin Martinson," he boomed, his deep voice filling the courtroom.

"How are you employed, sir?"

"I am a medical doctor," Martinson answered. "I currently work in the intensive care unit of Harborview Medical Center."

Brunelle nodded. "How long have you worked there?"

Martinson took a moment to think. "Eight years in June. I was at the University of Washington Medical Center for three years prior to that."

Brunelle didn't suppose he really needed to go through all of the good doctor's education and experience, but he didn't suppose it would hurt either. Milliken hadn't truly challenged any of the State's witnesses yet, but he would hate for Martinson to be the first and not have prepared against it by establishing the witness's expertise and bona fides.

"Could you tell us what education and experience you have to be able to do your current job?" he prompted.

"Of course." Martinson smiled. Most people liked talking about themselves. Brunelle had just required him not only to talk about himself, but to focus on his greatest accomplishments, and to do it to a packed gallery.

He went through his degrees and residencies, awards and fellowships. It was all very impressive, Brunelle was sure, although he stopped paying close attention after the name of his medical school. Brunelle guessed at least a few of the jurors did the same. In any event, after a few minutes, everyone in the courtroom knew Kevin Martinson was one heck of a doctor.

"Did you have occasion to treat a patient by the name of Harrison Jacoby?" Brunelle moved to the facts of his case.

"Yes, I did," Martinson confirmed.

"And how did that come about?" Brunelle invited.

Martinson had a natural ease about him. Without direction from Brunelle, he turned slightly and provided his answer directly to the jurors.

"Mr. Jacoby," he began, then corrected himself. "Dr. Jacoby. He's an M.D. too. Dr. Jacoby was brought to the emergency room with a gunshot wound to his head. Part of my duties in the ICU include assistance as needed and as possible in the emergency room. I was called down to assist in the evaluation and treatment of Dr. Jacoby."

"What were the nature and extent of his injuries when he arrived in the emergency room?" Brunelle moved along in his examination.

Martinson nodded again and turned to the jurors. "He

had suffered a gunshot wound to the head. Honestly, that's not usually a survivable injury. If the bullet penetrates the skull, it will cut a path through the brain. Most commonly, the bullet loses enough energy piercing the skull upon entry that it has insufficient energy to exit out the other side. The result is that it ricochets several times inside the skull, cutting multiple additional wound paths through the brain tissue."

"Is that what happened to Dr. Jacoby?" Brunelle asked.

"No," Martinson answered. "The angle of the gunshot wound was just enough that the bullet deflected off the base of his skull and failed to penetrate the bone."

"So, it just bounced off his skull?" Brunelle questioned.

"The bullet didn't simply bounce off," Martinson answered. "It fractured the skull significantly. The impact also fractured the cribriform plate, which is situated directly beneath the brain. All of this resulted in substantial cranial hemorrhaging."

"Is that dangerous?"

"It's very dangerous," Martinson answered. "It's often fatal."

"Was it fatal in this case?" Brunelle asked, as if he didn't know the answer.

Martinson frowned and shifted in his seat. "Not yet."

Brunelle liked that answer. "So, Dr. Jacoby is still alive?"

"He is," Martinson agreed hesitantly. "He is currently in a coma and being cared for in the ICU at Harborview."

"Will he survive?" Brunelle asked.

"Objection!" Milliken sprang to his feet. He had been so quiet up to that point in the trial, Brunelle had almost forgotten Milliken could object to his questions.

"The only thing relevant to this trial is that Dr. Jacoby is still alive," Milliken explained his objection. "Any speculation as to future medical outcomes runs the risk of confusing the issues to be presented to the jury."

"Any response, Mr. Brunelle?" Judge Parmenter invited.

Brunelle rubbed a hand over his chin. "I'll rephrase the question, Your Honor."

Parmenter nodded. "The objection is sustained."

Milliken sat down again and Brunelle asked a different, but similar question. "The injuries Dr. Jacoby suffered, those could have killed him, right?"

Martinson was no dummy. He gave Brunelle the answer he wanted. "They still might."

Before Milliken could object again, Brunelle announced, "No further questions."

Judge Parmenter looked to Milliken. "Any cross-examination?"

Milliken stood up again. "Yes, Your Honor. Thank you."

He stepped out from behind the defense counsel table and approached the witness stand in a slow, almost neighborly fashion.

"Dr. Martinson," he began, "it sounds like you've seen more than your fair share of gunshot wounds to the head."

Martinson shrugged. "When you work at the region's number one trauma center, you see a lot."

"Have you ever seen a shooting victim who was already dead from a gunshot wound to the head before you could even treat them?"

"D.O.A." Martinson nodded. "Dead on arrival. Yes, many times."

"And those are the cases you were talking about earlier," Milliken asked, "where the bullet bounced around inside the skull and turned the brain into Swiss cheese?"

"Those weren't the words I used," Martinson pointed out, "but that's not an inaccurate description."

"So, if I had a handgun, and I really wanted to kill someone," Milliken pantomimed pointing a pistol toward the ground, "I should shoot them directly in the back of the head to make sure the bullet penetrates the skull, is that correct?"

Martinson took a beat. "I'm not sure I mean to be giving advice on how to kill someone. My job is kind of the opposite of that."

"Well, let me ask it a different way, doctor," Milliken offered. "Would you agree with me that the gunshot to Harrison Jacoby was so poorly executed that it leads to the conclusion that the shooter didn't really want to kill him after all?"

Brunelle started to jump to his feet to object, but stopped himself. His urge to object was grounded in the fact that Milliken had asked a very good question that hurt Brunelle's case. If he objected, that was tantamount to shouting, 'Ouch!' in front of the jury. He would just have to rely on Martinson to help him out.

"I don't think I'm qualified to draw that conclusion," Martinson answered. "My job is to treat the patient, not guess as to the motives of his attacker."

Milliken nodded. "That's fair. Thank you, doctor. No further questions."

Milliken didn't need any further testimony from Martinson because it was his own question the jury would remember. Grunwald wasn't a bad shot, he was a merciful shot, unable to quite bring himself to murder his friend after all.

Brunelle hated it because it was smart.

"Any redirect-examination, Mr. Brunelle?" Judge Parmenter asked.

Martinson had weathered Milliken's cross-examination just fine. Brunelle had nothing he needed to rehabilitate him on.

"No, Your Honor," he answered. "This witness may be excused."

Dr. Martinson stepped down from the witness stand and exited the courtroom.

"Is the State ready to call its next witness?" the judge asked.

"Yes, Your Honor," Brunelle answered. The next witness was his too. "The State calls Detective Larry Chen to the stand."

CHAPTER 37

Chen knew the drill. He had been waiting in the hallway and stepped inside when he saw Martinson exit. Upon hearing Brunelle announce his name, he walked to the front of the courtroom and raised his right hand.

"Do you solemnly swear or affirm that your testimony will be the truth, the whole truth, and nothing but the truth?" Parmenter put to him.

"I do," Chen confirmed. He walked to the witness stand and sat down, ready for another question-and-answer session with Assistant District Attorney David Brunelle.

Brunelle took him through the basics. Name, rank, and badge number. Years with Seattle P.D., years as a detective, years handling major crimes and homicides. It was a lot. There was no question that Larry Chen was a grizzled old detective. He'd seen some things. And one of those things was the aftermath of William Grunwald trying to kill Harrison Jacoby.

"What did you see upon your arrival at the medical office of Grunwald and Jacoby?"

"By the time I arrived, patrol officers had already secured the scene," Chen turned to tell the jurors directly, just like they taught at the academy. "Dr. Jacoby had been taken to the hospital, and Dr. Grunwald was detained in the conference room."

"Did you speak with Dr. Grunwald?" Brunelle asked.

"I did," Chen confirmed with a nod.

"Did he tell you who shot Dr. Jacoby?"

"Yes." Chen turned again to the jury. "He confessed that he was the one who shot Dr. Jacoby."

Brunelle decided to let Milliken get into the why of it. Or rather, try to get into the why of it.

"No further questions, Your Honor."

Milliken stood up and accepted the judge's invitation to cross-examine the lead detective. He could hardly say no. The jury would never forgive him.

"Let's pick up where Mr. Brunelle left off," Milliken began. "You say my client confessed to shooting Dr. Jacoby. Did he also explain why he did so?"

"Objection." Brunelle stood up confidently. "Calls for hearsay."

Milliken pinched the bridge of his nose. "Are we really going to do this? Trials are supposed to be a search for the truth. My client will be testifying later in the trial anyway. There is no harm in allowing this witness to confirm that his version of events has been consistent."

"Let's do this the right way," Judge Parmenter said. He turned to Brunelle. "Please state the basis for your objection, Mr. Brunelle."

"The question calls for hearsay, Your Honor," Brunelle

explained. "The detective cannot testify as to what other people told him, including the defendant. If counsel wants to introduce that information to the jury, he can do so through his client, which he has repeatedly stated he intends to do."

Parmenter turned to Milliken. "How is this not hearsay, Mr. Milliken?"

Milliken pursed his lips. "I suppose it is hearsay, Your Honor. I just didn't think the prosecutor would try so hard to hide the truth from the jury."

"Yeah, I'm going to have to object to that, too, Your Honor," Brunelle spoke up. "If Mr. Milliken is going to impugn my integrity for insisting we all adhere to the evidence rules, perhaps we could do that outside the presence of the jury."

"All right, I think that's enough," Parmenter raised his hands at the lawyers. "Both of you. I will sustain the objection. You may not ask this witness to recount what someone else told him in order to prove the truth of that other person's statement. Ask another question."

Milliken stewed for several seconds, then suddenly regained himself. He snapped back into perfect posture and his usual confident smile popped onto his face. "I have no other questions for this witness, Your Honor. Thank you."

Brunelle had no redirect-exam, of course, and Chen was suddenly finished with his testimony ahead of schedule. That was fine with Brunelle. They were approaching the end of their case, and Milliken had failed to challenge any aspect of Chen's investigation. He really was putting all of his eggs in the basket of his client's testimony. He knew Brunelle would have no way to disprove whatever Grunwald said. That was why he wanted to give the jury a preview through Chen. When Brunelle blocked that, Milliken took his cross-examination ball and went home.

"Next witness?" Parmenter asked of the prosecutors.

It was Carlisle's turn to stand up again. "The State calls Detective Jack Houser to the stand."

CHAPTER 38

Houser was notably less comfortable testifying than Chen. He was a computer guy, not a people person. Chen made his living extracting information from witnesses and convincing bad guys to confess. Houser spent most of his time in a windowless tech lab. And when people did come to talk to him, he put trash cans on his desk.

When Carlisle announced Houser, Brunelle had to go out into the hallway to retrieve him. Once inside the courtroom, Brunelle had to tell him to go stand in front of the judge. And once he was there, the judge had to tell him to raise his right hand.

"Do you solemnly swear or affirm that the testimony you give will be the truth, the whole truth, and nothing but the truth?"

"Oh yes, Your Honor," Houser answered the judge's question. "Very much so, Your Honor."

Parmenter gestured toward the witness stand and, after a moment, Houser stepped over to it and sat down.

Brunelle wondered whether Houser had ever testified before. At least he seemed earnest.

"Please state your name for the record," Carlisle began. The same first question for every single witness.

"Jack Houser." He seemed pleased to have gotten the answer correct.

"How are you employed, Mr. Houser?" Carlisle continued the initial witness dance.

"I am a detective with the Seattle Police Department," Houser answered.

"Do you have an area of specialization or expertise?" Carlisle suggested.

Houser nodded. "Yes, I do. I specialize in forensic computer examination."

"What does that mean exactly?" Carlisle gestured to the jury box. Houser had been delivering all of his answers back to Carlisle. He must have been sick that day at the academy. "Can you explain it to the jury?"

"Oh, right. Yes. Of course." Houser made far too big a production out of turning in his seat and facing the jury. "Forensic computer examination is the practice of locating, preserving, extracting, and examining information stored in computer devices. Those devices include the traditional desktop and laptop computers, but cellular phones and tablets are also computers that I can examine."

Carlisle could have spent more time on the various types of examinations that could be performed on those different devices, but she elected to get right to the case at hand. Brunelle approved of the decision. Houser had valuable information, but he wasn't charming the jury any.

"Did you have occasion to examine any computer evidence in this case?" she prompted.

"More than one occasion," Houser answered.

"Okay," Carlisle nodded. She stepped over to the bailiff, one of whose many jobs was to store the exhibits until the lawyers were ready to use them in trial. She whispered to him, and after a moment, he produced a laptop from the shelves to his right. It was shiny and silver, with several stickers on it, including a yellow exhibit sticker.

Carlisle took the laptop and crossed back to the witness stand to hand it to Houser. "Is this the laptop you examined?"

Houser looked at the outside of the device, then nodded. "Yes."

"How do you know that?" Carlisle prompted.

"There's a label on it that says, 'Grunwald and Jacoby, Cosmetic Surgeons,'" Houser answered. "And it has a sticker I put on it with the police case number and my initials."

"Thank you, detective." Carlisle took the laptop back and returned it to the counter in front of the bailiff. "And what did you find when you examined that device?"

"Nothing." Houser grinned, obviously pleased with himself.

Carlisle seemed less pleased. "Nothing?"

"Exactly." Houser's smile broadened. "And that's something."

Carlisle sighed. "This is a trial, detective. Let's avoid clever turns of phrase if we can. Could you please explain the result of your examinations?"

Houser's grin faded. "Oh right. Sorry. Well, you see…" and he launched into a prop-less version of the explanation of how computer files that are ostensibly deleted are actually just stored elsewhere and remain retrievable by someone like him unless and until they are overwritten. "But in this case, the laptop contained absolutely no such files. They had all been purged."

"Were you able to tell when that occurred," Carlisle followed up, "in relation to the shooting?"

"I cross-referenced the metadata on the defendant's laptop with the recording of the 9-1-1 call," Houser answered. "The last file purge occurred three minutes after the defendant's call to 9-1-1 ended."

Nice. Brunelle nodded to himself. Houser was settling down, and his testimony made Grunwald look as shady as they knew he was.

"How is it possible to purge files so completely from a computer device?" Carlisle continued. "Can I go home and do that myself tonight with the laptop I bought from the big box computer store?"

Houser shook his head. "No. It takes a sophisticated level of software engineering to write a program that can do that thorough of a purge. You can't just download that from an app store."

"So, how would I obtain that?" Carlisle asked. Then refined it. "How would the defendant have obtained that?"

"We were able to identify and contact a local individual with the requisite ability to create such a program," Houser answered. "He was offering his services via internet chat rooms and using an alias."

"What was the alias?" Carlisle asked.

Houser actually remembered to look at the jury to deliver the answer. "The Owl."

Somehow, Houser's delivery came across as cool. A feat Brunelle found especially impressive given how uncool he found Barnaby.

"How did you find him?" Carlisle continued.

So, Houser provided an abbreviated version of the events

leading up to tracking down The Owl. "A slip of paper was found with the victim's belongings that had the words, '1900 OWL RD,' on it. At first it was thought that was a street address, 1900 Owl Road, but it was later determined to be an appointment time, person, and product. Seven p.m., The Owl, and the deletion program he called 'Real Delete.'"

"What did law enforcement do once that was determined?"

"We tracked down The Owl in one of the computer programmer chat rooms he frequented," Houser explained, "then engaged with him under the ruse of wanting to buy a copy of his Real Delete program."

"Did that actually work?" Carlisle asked.

"It did." Houser nodded.

"Why would he agree to meet with someone he didn't even know to sell them a product an average law-abiding citizen would have no need for?" Carlisle asked the question at least some of the jurors must have been thinking.

Houser provided the obvious answer. "Money."

"Of course," Carlisle remarked.

"And it wasn't cheap," Houser added. "There are few things more expensive than someone else's expertise."

Carlisle allowed a smile at that line, then continued. "So, did you just email him your credit card information and get an email with the deletion program attached?"

"Oh no." Houser chuckled. "No. The Owl wasn't going to accept payment or make delivery like that. It was a cash transaction, and the program was on a thumb drive."

"So, you had to meet in person?"

"Yes."

"And did you?"

"Yes, we did."

"What happened at that meeting?" Carlisle asked.

She should have been there, Brunelle thought with a small grin.

Houser took a moment to measure his answer. "The Owl was detained for questioning and identified."

That skipped over some of the less flattering details, Brunelle supposed, but it got to the point. Milliken could expand on cross-examination if he wanted to.

"What was The Owl's real name?" Carlisle inquired.

"Aiden Barnaby," Houser answered.

"And did Mr. Barnaby confirm," Carlisle followed up, "that he was the one who sold the deletion program to the defendant?"

Houser frowned slightly and shifted in his seat. "Well, as I said, we found the contact information for The Owl, er, Mr. Barnaby, in the victim's belongings. Not the defendant's."

Brunelle appreciated the detective's accuracy, even if he didn't like the uncertainty it injected into this aspect of the case.

"But yes," Houser continued. "The deletion program on the laptop was written by The Owl."

Carlisle nodded. "Thank you, Detective Houser. No further questions."

It was time for that cross-examination by Milliken. He accepted the judge's invitation and stood up as Carlisle sat down.

"Detective, you keep referring to the laptop you examined as my client's laptop," Milliken said as he slowly approached the witness. "But how do you know it was Dr. Grunwald's laptop if everything was deleted off of it?"

Houser nodded. "A very fair question. There are two ways, each equally valid in forensic police work. The first is that your client was the one who gave it to Detective Chen and said it was his. He even provided the passcode to unlock the user profile for the business. He wanted us to see that files had been purged. It was part of his defense, I guess."

Milliken had to nod. "I suppose it is," he allowed. "What was the second reason?"

"After we spoke with Mr. Barnaby," Houser answered, "I examined the laptop again and located a second hidden user profile that was a private profile just for your client."

Brunelle dropped his pen and looked at Carlisle. She seemed as surprised as him.

Milliken was caught off guard as well. "I'm sorry. What?"

"When you turn the laptop on," Houser explained, "it prompts you to enter the passcode for the business profile. That was the passcode the defendant willingly provided. After speaking with Mr. Barnaby and confirming there were specially purchased secrecy programs installed on the device, I hard-started it to see if I could locate any additional user profiles that might be on it. Sure enough there was a second profile."

"But how can you know that second user profile was associated with Dr. Grunwald?" Milliken challenged. "Didn't you just testify that it was Dr. Jacoby who purchased the deletion program?"

"We believe it was Dr. Jacoby," Houser qualified. "But as for the second user profile, it was labeled 'WDG,' which are Dr. Grunwald's initials. The passcode was the digits of his birth date, but in reverse order. I feel confident it's his profile."

"How did you determine the passcode?" Milliken challenged.

Houser shrugged. "Most people use some variation on an important date. It has to be something they can remember, right?

I've done this before. I always start with birthdays. I don't usually need very many attempts. I didn't with this one either."

Brunelle glanced again at his co-counsel. She stuck out an impressed lower lip and nodded at Houser's initiative.

Then Milliken had to ask the question everyone in the courtroom was wondering. If he didn't, he would look like he was afraid of it, and Carlisle would definitely ask it on redirect. "What did you find under this second user profile?"

Houser shook his head. "Nothing. And again, that was something. All of the files stored under that user profile had also been deleted using the same program."

Milliken took a moment. Brunelle knew he was weighing whether to probe further and potentially uncover additional evidence that made Grunwald look shady, or be grateful the damage hadn't been greater and sit down. The choice was clear.

"No further questions, Your Honor."

Milliken returned to his seat and Carlisle popped out of hers.

"This second user profile," she began, "would it be visible as a sign-in option when the computer was first turned on?"

Houser shook his head. "Not unless you knew it was there and wanted to use it. It only comes up as an option if you hold down the 'control' and 'function' buttons as the device powers on."

Carlisle nodded. "Thank you, Detective Houser. Nothing further."

"Any recross-examination based on that question, Mr. Milliken?" Judge Parmenter asked.

Milliken stood up and shook his head. "No, Your Honor. Dr. Grunwald will provide further explanation when he testifies."

That was inappropriate, Brunelle thought disapprovingly.

Parmenter didn't seem to appreciate the theatrics either, but refrained from admonishing Milliken in front of the jury. Instead, he excused the witness and recessed the proceedings for a fifteen-minute break.

"I feel like that went pretty well," Carlisle whispered to Brunelle as people began filtering out of the courtroom.

Brunelle agreed. "Even better than I expected."

"I wonder what that secret profile was for?" Carlisle mused.

"Milliken will figure out a way to wrap it into his duress claim," Brunelle expected.

"At some point," Carlisle said, "the jury has to see that Grunwald is lying."

"That point will come soon enough," Brunelle replied. "We're down to our last witness. Come on, let's see if The Owl is in the hallway."

CHAPTER 39

Aiden 'The Owl' Barnaby was indeed waiting in the hallway outside the courtroom. He was seated on a bench next to his lawyer, Jessica Edwards. She stood up when Brunelle and Carlisle emerged.

"Does Aiden go on after the break?" she asked.

"Yep." Brunelle nodded. "He's our last witness."

"How has it gone?" Edwards nodded toward the courtroom. "Are you going to get him? I mean, generally I root against you guys, but I want the best possible result for my client."

"Well enough," Carlisle offered her opinion. "Your guy better sell it. We want to finish strong."

"Finishing strong would be putting the victim on," Edwards replied, "but he's still in no condition for that, right?"

"He's in the worst possible condition," Brunelle said. "Too unconscious to testify, too not dead to knock out Grunwald's duress defense."

"Very sensitive." Edwards frowned. "Work that into your

closing argument."

"I will," Carlisle put in. "Plus anything useful your client gives us. He better give us some useful answers."

Edwards grinned. "Then I guess you better ask some useful questions."

* * *

"The State calls Aiden Barnaby to the stand." Brunelle made the announcement after everyone had reconvened in the courtroom and Judge Parmenter prompted the State to call its next witness.

Barnaby was already seated in the back of the courtroom, again next to Edwards. She gestured for him to go forward and be sworn in by the judge. He walked forward wearing a navy suit that looked like it still had the tags on it. When he reached the judge's bench, he raised his right hand, swore to tell the truth, the whole truth, and nothing but the truth. Then he took the stand and Brunelle took the reins.

"Please state your name for the record," he began.

But Barnaby hesitated right out of the gate. "Uh, my real name, or…?"

"Your legal name, yes," Brunelle confirmed. "We'll get to your other monicker in a minute."

"Okay." Barnaby nodded. "Aiden Michael Barnaby."

"How are you employed, Mr. Barnaby?"

Again, hesitation. "My main job, or…?"

"Main job," Brunelle confirmed. "We'll get to your side hustle in a minute too. What is your profession?"

"Oh, I'm a computer software engineer," Barnaby answered.

"Who is your main employer?" Brunelle asked in a way he hoped Barnaby wouldn't question.

"MegaThink," Barnaby answered. "I work at their Fremont campus."

"Okay, and do you also do," Brunelle sought the best word, "freelance programming work?"

Barnaby nodded stiffly. "Yes."

"What is the nature of that freelance work?" Brunelle prompted.

Barnaby shifted in his seat. "Uh, I can write programs for things you can't really buy at the store, if you know what I mean."

"I think I do," Brunelle replied, "but I don't know if the jury does. Can you explain what kind of programs you're talking about?"

Barnaby looked cautiously at the jurors without turning his body to face them. "Illegal stuff." He just went ahead and said it. "The kind of stuff you use to delete evidence from your computer."

Brunelle liked that answer. It was more forthright than he'd expected.

"And that's why I can't buy it at the store?" Brunelle followed up. "That's why I have to find someone like you?"

"There aren't a lot of people like me," Barnaby answered, reminding Brunelle why he didn't like him very much.

"Okay," Brunelle accepted the answer. "And to do this side hustle selling illegal computer programs, do you use your legal name or another name, as you alluded to earlier?"

"I use an alias," Barnaby confirmed.

"What's that alias?"

Barnaby looked again to the jurors. "The Owl," he said, as if it were his superhero code name.

Brunelle had to ask finally. "Why 'The Owl'?"

Barnaby lifted his chin and narrowed his eyes. "Because

owls fly in the black of night and see things others don't."

"Wow. Okay." Brunelle hated that. "So, Owl, if I want to hire you to scrub my computer of all of the evidence that I've been embezzling from my company, how do I do that? I assume you don't have ads on the sides of busses or anything like that."

"I get contacted through online message boards," Barnaby answered. "You have to get my name from someone else."

"Or from you, right?" Brunelle said. "Didn't you refer me and my team to The Owl without telling us that was really you?"

Barnaby laughed slightly. "Yeah, I did that."

"Why would you do that?"

"Government money is still money," Barnaby answered.

"And you thought you could outsmart us," Brunelle added.

Barnaby shrugged. "I might still."

Brunelle did not like that answer. He didn't suppose the jury did either.

"Great. Let's move on," he responded. "Did you sell an illicit file deletion program to someone related to this case?"

"I guess so," Barnaby answered. "That's why I'm here, right? Some doctor or something?"

"Cosmetic surgeons, yes," Brunelle confirmed. "You probably don't collect customer names, do you?"

Barnaby shook his head. "I just collect their money."

Brunelle stepped over to the exhibits in front of the bailiff and selected two photographs sitting there next to the laptop.

"For the record," he said, "I'm showing you photographs of two individuals. Have you seen these photographs before?"

"Yeah, you showed me these when you guys questioned me," Barnaby revealed, accepting the photos from Brunelle.

"And you were able to identify which of these two cosmetic surgeons you met with to sell the deletion program," Brunelle reminded him. "Isn't that correct?"

"I guess so." Barnaby shrugged again. "I think it was more like I thought it probably wasn't this guy." He held up the photograph of Grunwald. "But it was a while ago, and it was dark. I wasn't trying to memorize faces or anything."

Brunelle pointed at the photo Barnaby was holding up, then at Grunwald. "Does that appear to be a photograph of the man seated at the defendant's table?"

Barnaby looked from the photograph to Grunwald and back again. "Yeah, I guess so."

"And you don't recall ever selling him a file deletion program?"

"Not that I recall," Barnaby answered.

"So, if he said he bought such a program from you in order to delete threatening emails he received from unknown internet blackmailers demanding he murder his business partner for no known reason," Brunelle laid out Grunwald's defense in the most ridiculous terms, "that would be a lie. Right?"

Barnaby just sat there for several seconds. "I don't know about all that. I just sell this stuff on the side to pay for some habits that can be pretty expensive, you know? I'm just trying to make a few bucks."

"I do know," Brunelle answered. "It's my job to know. Like your job is to help people forever delete evidence of crimes."

"Yeah, I mean, nothing is really forever," Barnaby defended. "Even my program doesn't always get everything. Computers are complex. They hide stuff all over the place." He pointed to the exhibits by the bailiff. "I could probably find something on that laptop still, if I really wanted to. Especially if it's a different filetype than I programmed for."

Brunelle froze for a moment. That was definitely not on his list of prepared questions for Barnaby, but he was hardly going to pass up that invitation.

"Okay." Brunelle retrieved the laptop from the bailiff and handed it to Barnaby. "Try to find something."

Milliken stood up. "I'm going to object, Your Honor. This is nothing more than theater. The computer has already been examined, and its files were in exactly the condition Dr. Grunwald said they would be. Further examination by Mr. 'Owl' is not evidence. It's a desperate trick by a desperate prosecutor who knows he has failed to prove the charges against my client."

"Now who's doing theater, Mr. Milliken?" Judge Parmenter admonished. He looked down to Brunelle. "Any response to the objection?"

"I'm not even sure what the legal objection is, Your Honor," Brunelle answered. "It seems to be a relevance objection, but this witness has the expertise to look at the defendant's laptop and determine whether there might be overlooked evidence in the case. I can't think of anything more relevant."

"I agree," Parmenter said. "Objection overruled. You may proceed, Mr. Brunelle."

"Please turn the laptop on, Mr. Barnaby," Brunelle directed. "Oh, and when you do, hold down the control and function keys."

Barnaby nodded at the instructions and powered up the laptop. After a minute or two, he looked up. "I need the passcode."

Brunelle returned to the prosecution table and picked up a police report. They always listed the suspect's personal identifiers. "Try this," he said and read the numbers on

Grunwald's birth date in reverse order.

Barnaby typed the digits then nodded. "That worked. I'm in."

"How long will it take you," Brunelle asked, "to determine whether there might be a remnant of a threatening email somewhere on that device?"

"It'll be quicker if you stop talking to me," Barnaby replied, eyes intent on the screen as his fingers clacked furiously against the keyboard.

Brunelle decided to let the comment pass. He turned to Carlisle who only offered an amused smirk.

Milliken stood up again. "Perhaps we should take a recess, Your Honor?"

"No, no." Barnaby raised a hand at him. "I'm almost done."

Brunelle returned his attention to Barnaby. His eyes did take on an owl-like quality, lit up by the glow of the laptop. Then those eyes suddenly widened. Brunelle thought maybe The Owl found something—and he really hoped it wasn't one of the emails Grunwald claimed—but then Barnaby slammed the laptop shut.

"Nope. Nothing," he announced. "I was wrong. Can I go now?"

"You are not excused, Mr. Barnaby," Judge Parmenter informed him. "The lawyers have more questions for you, I'm sure."

Brunelle wasn't sure he did have any more questions. Barnaby had given him what he wanted, plus a little excitement. He decided to quit while he was ahead.

"I have no further questions, Your Honor," he said. "I imagine Mr. Milliken might have a few."

Brunelle returned to his seat and looked forward to seeing how Barnaby held up under cross-examination. Milliken stood again and came out from behind the defense table like a tiger emerging from the trees.

"So, let me make sure I understand," he began. "You are a computer programmer who uses a fake name to help people hide evidence of their crimes; you lied to the police and prosecutors in the hopes of earning a few more dollars; and now you sit here and claim that you sold a file deletion program to my client or his business partner. Is all of that correct?"

"I don't know who is whose business partner," Barnaby answered. "But the rest of that is correct. And yes, I can tell you, my program is on that laptop."

Milliken clasped his hands behind his back and nodded sternly several times. Then he threw his hands in front of him and clapped. "Well, that sounds like exactly what my client told the police. Thank you, Mr. Barnaby. It's been a pleasure to meet you." Then, to the judge, "I have no further questions, Your Honor."

Brunelle frowned at Milliken's antics, but he was relieved his opponent chose that route rather than a long and arduous takedown of the State's final witness, with special emphasis on the sweet plea bargain he was getting for being a snitch.

"Any redirect-examination, Mr. Brunelle?" Parmenter inquired.

"No, Your Honor," Brunelle responded.

Judge Parmenter looked down at Barnaby. "Now you are excused, sir."

Barnaby practically jumped off the witness stand and rushed out of the courtroom, Edwards hurrying after him.

"Does the State have any further witnesses?" Parmenter directed his question at both of the prosecutors.

Brunelle stood to answer it. "No, Your Honor. The State rests."

Parmenter nodded, then looked to the jurors. "Ladies and gentlemen of the jury, that concludes the presentation of the State's evidence." He looked at the clock on the wall. The day wasn't nearly over, but there was a standard professional courtesy to adjourn the case until the next day to allow both attorneys to prepare for the defense case to begin fresh in the morning. "I have some scheduling matters to discuss with the attorneys, so we will adjourn for the day and reconvene first thing in the morning for further proceedings. Thank you."

The 'scheduling matters' in question were just confirming that Milliken still intended to put Grunwald on the stand. A criminal defendant did not have to testify, no matter how many times their lawyer told the jury they would. Parmenter just wanted to confirm Grunwald still intended to take the stand, but he couldn't say that in front of the jury in case the answer was no.

Parmenter formally recessed the trial for the day, and the courtroom emptied, first of court staff, then Milliken and Grunwald, then the last of the spectators. Eventually, Brunelle and Carlisle were alone, packing up the last of their materials.

"That Owl guy is weird," Carlisle said. "I don't know if the jury liked him."

"Probably not," Brunelle guessed. "But he gave us what we needed."

"He thinks pretty highly of himself." Carlisle laughed. She picked up the laptop from near the bailiff's station. "Not only can he write a program that permanently deletes everything, he can also undelete it. But just him. He's that good. He's The Owl."

"Hoot," Brunelle joked.

Carlisle opened the laptop. "I wonder what Grunwald's

desktop wallpaper is. Probably something douchey."

Brunelle laughed and stepped over to see himself. Carlisle held down the control and function keys, but it wasn't necessary. Barnaby hadn't logged out of Grunwald's secret profile. They saw the image he left on Grunwald's desktop.

Carlisle raised a hand to cover her gaping mouth.

Brunelle reached out and closed the laptop. "Oh, shit."

CHAPTER 40

The next morning, Judge Parmenter looked down at Milliken and asked formally, "Does the defense wish to call any witnesses?"

Milliken stood and answered with a similar air of artifice. "We do, Your Honor. The defense calls the accused, Dr. William Grunwald."

A subdued murmur rippled through the packed courtroom. While there was certainly some drama in the calling of the defendant to the stand, some of it had been bled away by Millikin repeatedly promising the moment. But the foreknowledge that the day would start with the defendant's testimony led to a standing-room only crowd. News cameras lined the back wall, attorneys of all stripes filled the middle rows, and Mrs. Elizabeth Grunwald and Mrs. Veronica Jacoby once again occupied their respective seats in the front row.

Brunelle forced himself not to scan the crowd to see if

Marietta Lang was watching. He hadn't seen or heard from her since standing her up that night at GlasHaus.

The man accused of attempted murder walked up to the judge presiding over his trial and swore the same oath as any other witness.

"Do you solemnly swear or affirm the testimony you give in this proceeding will be the truth, the whole truth, and nothing but the truth?"

Grunwald nodded. "Yes, I do, Your Honor."

"You may take the witness stand," Parmenter directed. Then, to Milliken, "Whenever you're ready, counsel."

Milliken waited for his client to get comfortable—as comfortable as a defendant on the witness stand could get—and began his examination.

"Good morning, sir. Could you please tell us your name?"

Grunwald turned to jurors. He'd learned from the cops, or, more likely, been instructed by his lawyer. "My name is William Douglas Grunwald."

Brunelle fiddled with the pen he should have been taking notes with. As dramatic as it was to call a defendant to the stand, there was nothing more electric than when the prosecutor stood to cross-examine the defendant. The courtroom would crackle with the anticipation of the first question out of Brunelle's mouth. And he could hardly contain himself waiting for that opportunity.

Normally, he would pay extreme attention to every word the defendant uttered, calculating exactly how to use it against him in an aggressive and relentless cascade of inquiries and challenges designed to reveal unequivocally the defendant's guilt. But Brunelle couldn't have cared less what Grunwald claimed on direct examination. None of it mattered. Brunelle had cracked the case, and he just needed to wait his turn to reveal what had really happened that night at the offices of Grunwald and Jacoby.

There were a few subjects where Brunelle was curious how Grunwald would explain them away. Why would Jacoby buy the deletion software for Grunwald to conceal the plot to kill him? The answer? He didn't. Barnaby was just wrong.

"I'm not sure why Mr. Barnaby thought he sold the program to Harry," Grunwald told the jurors, "but I'm the one who bought it from him. Right there under the Fremont Bridge."

The late nights, and extra money, both his and Jacoby's wives had noticed.

"I had no reason to be angry with Harry. We'd never been more successful. I guess we just had more clients than ever. That happens when word gets out that you're the best."

Why he told the 9-1-1 operator it was a robbery gone wrong wasn't so clear.

"The blackmailers told me I had to make it look like someone else did it, but I didn't know how to do that. When the police arrived, I knew they would know I did it."

At least that last part was true, Brunelle thought.

He also went into remarkably minute detail about the number, length, content, and times of the emails he claimed to have received. And also that he created the second, secret user profile on the laptop so Jacoby wouldn't know about what was on it.

That was true too, Brunelle knew, but not for the reasons Grunwald claimed.

Eventually, Milliken had led his client expertly through a forest of lies so detailed and dense, the jury might well conclude the story had to be true, if only because no one could possibly lie that much.

But Brunelle was a professional. He'd spent a career listening to the lies of murderers.

"Is there anything else you want the jurors to know," Milliken brought his examination to a close, "before I finish my questions, Dr. Grunwald?"

The good doctor turned again to the jury box. "Just that Harry was my best friend. We spent our lives creating a shared dream. I would never do anything to hurt him. I love him. But I love my son more. I was so afraid these people would harm Kaeden, maybe even kill him. I'm still afraid they will because I'm telling people what they did."

He wiped at eyes that looked pretty dry to Brunelle.

"I was so scared for Kaeden, and I had to make a choice. I wish I never pulled that trigger. But I hope you can understand why I did."

Milliken nodded solemnly as his client finished the undoubtedly scripted and rehearsed conclusion to his testimony.

"I hope so, too, Bill," he said, allowing his voice to crack. "I think they will."

He took a moment, then looked up to Judge Parmenter and offered one more solemn nod. "I have no further questions for Dr. Grunwald, Your Honor. Thank you."

And it was finally Brunelle's turn.

"Destroy him," Carlisle whispered as he stood up.

He had every intention to.

"Any cross-examination, Mr. Brunelle?" Parmenter asked.

"Oh, yes," Brunelle answered as he stormed out from behind the prosecution table. He walked straight at Grunwald. There were various distances a lawyer could stand from a witness depending on how supportive or challenging the lawyer wanted to be. Generally, the farther away the lawyer stood, the more supportive, and the closer, the more aggressive. Brunelle marched to the closest spot any lawyer would stand when confronting a witness, then took one step more.

"I don't care about any of what you just said," he started, waving a hand in the air. "It's all a bunch of lies. You're just a coward. You couldn't even pull the trigger right."

"Objection!" Milliken jumped to his feet to defend his client. "That's not cross-examination. That's just badgering the witness."

Judge Parmenter leaned down at Brunelle. "Do you have a question, counsel?"

Brunelle nodded up to the judge. "Sure, I've got some questions."

He turned back to Grunwald and fired off a list of questions, answering all but the last one himself.

"What illegal activity were you and Jacoby doing that led to so many late nights and so much extra money? Selling excess drugs or confidential patient information, I bet."

"Whose idea was it to use a dedicated laptop, not connected to the main computer, to keep track of the illegal activities? Jacoby. You're too dumb to think of that."

"Which of you convinced the other that you needed a permanent way to delete evidence of whatever you were doing? You. I know it was you."

"When did you realize you could set up a second user profile on that laptop and use the deletion software for your own sick purposes? Probably before you even bought it."

Grunwald sat stone silent, staring at Brunelle, his eyes widening with each question.

"And finally…" Brunelle walked over and retrieved the laptop from the bailiff again. He powered it up, holding the control and function keys, then entered Grunwald's birth date in reverse. When the login completed, he spun it around so Grunwald could see what Barnaby had managed to recover the day before. "Is this the same child porn image Jacoby saw on the laptop when you forgot to log out of your secret profile, and you decided you had to kill him to keep your secret safe? Or was it one of the hundreds of others you deleted when you were done looking at them?"

If the courtroom had been quiet waiting for the first question, it was beyond silent waiting for the last answer.

"Answer the question, Grunwald," Brunelle growled.

Grunwald dropped his head into his hands. "I panicked! He wasn't supposed to see that. He was going to tell my wife, or the police, or someone. He was going to tell someone.

"I grabbed my gun out of my office and came up behind him while he was looking to see what else I had on there. I pulled the trigger, but I flinched. He was my best friend. But then there was blood everywhere, and he wasn't moving, and I was sure he was dead. I called 9-1-1 and told them it was a robbery gone bad. But I realized I didn't know how to make it look like a robbery, not before the cops got there.

"Then I remembered a T.V. show I saw where a guy was being blackmailed by bad guys who had video of his kid leaving school, and I thought that might work. I deleted everything off the laptop before the cops got there and then told them it was all the emails I deleted."

He shook his head, real tears streaking his cheeks. Brunelle knew the tears were for himself.

"I'm sorry," he pleaded. "I'm so, so sorry."

Brunelle shook his head. "Tell it to the judge."

Then he walked over to the defense table and looked Seattle's best criminal defense attorney dead in the eye. "No further questions."

EPILOGUE

The sentencing hearing was two weeks later. Grunwald didn't plead guilty, even after his confession. But Milliken didn't offer any further evidence; closing arguments were minimal; and the jury returned the guilty verdict by the end of the day.

When they got back up to Brunelle's office, Carlisle slapped him on the back. "Well done, counselor. Twenty years in prison isn't enough for that guy."

"We'll add ten years when Jacoby dies," Brunelle replied. "Veronica said, now that they have some closure, the family is gathering next week to remove life support. Then we'll resentence him on murder."

Carlisle was about to say something when there came a rap on Brunelle's door frame. It was Marietta Lang. "Sorry to interrupt. It's my last day here." She held up the document in her hand. "I thought you might want to see my report. And I wanted to say goodbye."

Carlisle jabbed a thumb toward the exit. "I'm just going to leave now. And hope I'm not getting laid off."

"You're not," Lang assured her. "No one is. I learned the

people leading this office have the highest ethics. Despite my best efforts," she added with a laugh. "I wouldn't change a thing here."

Carlisle departed with a sigh of relief. Brunelle thanked Lang and wished her well with a firm handshake and nothing more. Then it was time to go home. There was one last loose end related to the case that needed to be tied up. And he needed some time to prepare.

When Casey got home from work, not only was dinner on the table, but so were the candles and a bucket of ice with a bottle of not inexpensive champagne in it. Brunelle was in his best suit.

"Wow." Casey chuckled as Brunelle kissed her on the cheek and guided her into the dining room.

Their dining room.

"What's the occasion?" she asked.

"An anniversary, I hope," Brunelle answered.

Casey cocked her head at him. "What does that mean?"

"You lost the bet," Brunelle said, "but you never should have had to make that bet, and I never should have taken it. I'd already won. I was just too scared to accept it. But I'm not scared anymore."

He took Casey's left hand in his, then lowered himself onto one knee and pulled the ring out of his jacket pocket.

"Casey Emory, would you do me the immeasurable honor of becoming my wife?"

Casey took the ring, then pulled Brunelle back to his feet by the knot of his tie and kissed him long and hard.

"You're damn right I will."

END

246   *Stephen Penner*

THE DAVID BRUNELLE LEGAL THRILLERS
Presumption of Innocence
Tribal Court
By Reason of Insanity
A Prosecutor for the Defense
Substantial Risk
Corpus Delicti
Accomplice Liability
A Lack of Motive
Missing Witness
Diminished Capacity
Devil's Plea Bargain
Homicide in Berlin
Premeditated Intent
Alibi Defense
Defense of Others
Necessity
The Interests of Justice
Under Duress

THE TALON WINTER LEGAL THRILLERS
Winter's Law
Winter's Chance
Winter's Reason
Winter's Justice
Winter's Duty
Winter's Passion

THE RAIN CITY LEGAL THRILLERS
Burden of Proof
Trial by Jury
The Survival Rule
Double Jeopardy
Prime Suspects
Body of Evidence
Judge and Jury

ABOUT THE AUTHOR

Stephen Penner is an author, artist, and attorney from Seattle, Washington. He has written more than 35 novels and specializes in courtroom thrillers known for their unexpected twists and candid portrayal of the justice system. He draws on his extensive experience as a criminal trial attorney to infuse his writing with realism and insight.

Stephen is the author of several top-rated legal thriller series. *The David Brunelle Legal Thrillers* feature Seattle homicide D.A. David Brunelle and a recurring cast of cops, defense attorneys, and forensic experts. *The Talon Winter Legal Thrillers* star tough-as-nails Tacoma criminal defense attorney Talon Winter. And *The Rain City Legal Thrillers* deliver the adventures of attorney Daniel Raine and his unlikely partner, real estate agent/private investigator Rebecca Sommers.

For more information, please visit *www.stephenpenner.com*.